CAROLINE'S CHOICE

HEARTS IN WINTER BOOK 4

SIMONE BEAUDELAIRE

This book is dedicated to Gabrielle, Adrienne, Ian and Alyssa.
Thank you for making me a mom.

CHAPTER 1

*V*ictor Martinez paused in front of the office of his favorite professor, Dr. Caroline Jones.

He had taken all four of his English classes from her, and even though he had long since completed his English requirements, he liked to stop by and say hello now and again. Caring and involved beyond what her job required, Dr. Jones always seemed more like a friend than a teacher. *My days of stopping by to see her are drawing to a close,* he thought with a pang, *but I can't resist visiting one more time…and one more…and probably one more after that.*

He sighed, reading a notice on the door inviting students to contribute to the literary magazine. *If I had the cojones to write it, I could sure add a contribution to that… but it would reveal too much and probably embarrass her.* He sighed, terminal shyness warring with desperate longing.

I should quit hanging around. I don't even have a reason to be in the Humanities building anymore.

None of his meandering thoughts stopped him from lifting his hand to knock.

Through the closed door, he heard Caroline's normally musical voice raised to nearly a shout, angry and tinged with grief. The sound froze his movement colder than the frost outside the window. He'd never heard such a tone from her before.

"No, and that's final," she snarled, and then, a moment later, "No, it was your responsibility to make sure I knew how you felt since you…" her voice broke, "you were the one with the unusual priorities."

After a long pause punctuated by rasping breaths loud enough to penetrate the door, she snarled, "It's over, William. Don't contact me again."

The telephone clanged into the receiver loudly enough Victor could hear it from the hallway. Shattered respirations told the rest of the story.

The sound drew Victor like a magnet. Unable to consider any alternatives, he knocked gently and opened the door without waiting for a reply.

The move revealed a cozy, feminine space containing a desk topped with a purple and blue scarf, long fringes trailing over the edges. Behind and to the left stood two bookshelves loaded with textbooks and novels. To the right, a cream leather loveseat took up the entire wall. Framed sketches of Robert Browning and Elizabeth Barrett Browning hung above it.

Caroline sat behind her desk, her face buried in her hands, shoulders shaking. At his entrance, her head shot up, revealing a red nose and tears streaming down her cheeks.

Victor stepped into the room and shut the door behind him. "Hello, Dr. Jones," he said gently.

"Victor." She tried to smile. It wasn't convincing at all.

"What's wrong?" he asked, unable to suppress his growing concern.

"I suppose you wouldn't believe me if I said nothing was wrong." She smiled, an unsteady twisting of her lips that revealed no humor.

Victor just looked at her.

"It's personal," she added finally.

"Yes, I can see that," he replied, "but it's not good to be alone when personal things are going wrong. Is there anyone I can call for you?"

She considered for a moment. "No, not really."

What is that in her expression? Like… desperation. She must want to let it out. "Then could you talk to me?" he urged. "I don't like to see you hurting like this."

"Don't you think it's a little unprofessional? After all, you're still a student, right?" Something in her tone seemed to ask him to keep probing, not to take the immediate rejection as final.

"Yes," he admitted. "I have one more semester after this one. However, I'm not *your* student anymore. I never will be again, so I don't think we have to worry about that." He took a breath, reaching across the desk to lay his hand on hers. "I would rather be your friend."

Caroline smiled, a little more convincingly this time.

She likes that idea too. Excellent. Maybe I can cultivate a more personal connection with her over time.

"Please, come sit with me," she urged. "Personal conversations shouldn't take place across a desk." She indicated the sofa as she rose, settling onto the cushions and wiping her eyes with one finger as though to dispel any lingering wetness.

.Lord, she's beautiful, he thought, admiring her glossy, chocolate-colored hair clipped into a pixie cut that looked both sexy and innocent, her hazel eyes glowing even greener than usual. Victor's heart began hammering as he crossed the room in three small steps. *I can hardly believe how bold I was, pushing this conversation on her. Everyone knows how shy I am… but this is Dr. Jones. There's something about her that has always dragged me into action. Besides, if there's a human being who knows my innermost thoughts better than this woman, I can't imagine who it would be.*

A closeness exists between a nurturing teacher and a responsive student that transcends gender and age.

3

After four semesters—two full years—of him writing with more and more openness, Victor had become a book laid open on her desk, and she had read every page.

The bond went both directions, too. A teacher reveals feelings, likes and dislikes, and aspects of character. An astute observer can pick up on these cues and come to know the person behind the podium. Victor had observed Caroline closely. The step between student and friend was one of definition only.

They sat in silence for several seconds. Silence didn't bother him, and it was a comfortable kind of quiet anyway, one that meant she didn't feel nervous with him there.

"There's really nothing too shocking," she said at last. "I broke up with my boyfriend. We've been together for almost three years. It was the right thing to do, but it still hurts."

"What went wrong?" he asked, letting every ounce of concern bleed into his expression.

"I… well… I'm thirty-three years old, Victor. I want a family. When I started to talk to him about marriage, children, he said he wasn't interested in either one, ever. He figured on remaining single for life. I couldn't live with that. We have different goals and priorities. I guess we really don't belong together…" Caroline sniffled and rubbed her reddened nose.

'What kind of jackass is this? He doesn't want to get married? Have kids? What was he hanging around so long for?'

"I guess I just let him," she replied, shoulders drooping. "We dated casually for a year before becoming… close. Then I assumed things were progressing, and he apparently didn't. I let our relationship drift too long, and it's three years later. I'm no closer to having a family and…" she sniffled.

4

Victor took her hand in his. "And..." he prodded gently.

"And now I probably never will." Her face turned bleak with grief.

"Why on earth not?" He stared at her, puzzled.

Seeming to realize his confusion, she inhaled a deep breath and blurted, "I'm over thirty with no prospects. Making a family is a slow process. Even if I met someone right away, it would take time... too much time, and by then, the risks increase of either not being able to have a child, or of having one with... problems."

She isn't wrong, but there has to be a solution. Victor considered, his eyes roving over her lovely face. An idea dawned on him... *but how to phrase it... it's a personal suggestion and I don't want her to take offense.* "Well," he said slowly, carefully squashing down any feelings his words might generate, "if you insist on doing everything the traditional way, you may be right. After all, you have to meet someone, fall in love, get engaged, plan a wedding, and then get pregnant. That could take years. But what if you decided not to go the traditional route?"

Her delicately arched eyebrows drew together. "What do you mean?"

"Well, what if you asked a friend to help you get pregnant? Then you could have a baby right away and work on the rest later." Years of pretending he didn't go through life squirming with shyness enabled Victor to say the words, but the heat in his face sufficed to tell him his suggestion didn't sound as casual as he'd hoped.

Her eyes widened and then narrowed, but she answered the suggestion, not his expression. "I wouldn't even know where to start. Who would be willing to do that?"

"You might be surprised, Caroline." It felt both strange and exciting to use her first name. His detachment melted away like snow in April with each word, until he spoke directly from the heart. "You are one of the kindest people I know. You should be able to have as many babies as you want. You would be a wonderful mother. What a fool your William is not to realize what he had."

She rewarded him with pink cheeks and shy half-smile. "You're sweet, Victor, but I think you're overestimating my charms. No one I know would do such a thing for me. I wouldn't even know how to ask."

The discussion distracted her from her misery. Good. But it also opened a door for me. Victor took a deep breath and steeled himself. He couldn't *not* take the next step. *The risk is great, but the reward…*He brought up one calloused hand to touch her face, and he said softly, his voice husky with feeling, "I'm not overestimating anything."

Caroline's eyes widened.

He continued. "You have no idea how desirable you are, do you? Well, little teacher, let me show you. I'm going to kiss you, right now. Stop me." He leaned forward with aching slowness.

She didn't stop him.

His lips caressed Caroline's with the same tentative desire he was sure she'd heard in his voice.

Her hands came up against his chest, not to push him away, but just to touch. The warmth of her fingers sank through the soft gray fabric of his tee-shirt and seemed to brand his skin.

When he pulled back, she opened her eyes slowly. "Did you actually want me to stop you?"

"Of course not," he replied, his eyes intense and hot as they burned into hers, "but I wanted to give you fair warning."

"Why?"

"Why what? Please don't be asking why I kissed you!"

6

"Why now, Victor? Why today? Please say you aren't just feeling sorry for me."

"No, Caroline, nothing like that. I've wanted to forever, since my freshman year. I've dreamed about you. Today seemed like the right day. I might never have another opportunity like this, and I'm not a fool."

"It's a lot to take in. You were a student to me yesterday." Yet her expression hinted at something... more.

"Not just another student," he dared to press.

"No," she admitted, her eyes skating away from his. Then she looked back, meeting his gaze. "A really important one. You have always been terribly special to me, but the distinction still matters. I could be in so much trouble for just that kiss." She gulped. "This has been a horrible day, and now... What do you want from me?"

"Only for you to be happy," he replied with all honesty. "You work so hard helping others. You deserve it. If I can play some part in it, I will. I want to. Also, I want to kiss you again. You had better stop me this time," he challenged her.

~

Caroline gazed into Victor's beautiful brown eyes. More desire than she had ever had directed at her before set them ablaze. She found herself susceptible to that lust, that longing. *If I'm honest, I have to admit I've never been completely immune to it. Plus, his first kiss was absolutely delicious.* "No, don't stop."

This time he moved with deliberation. His arms encircled her slim waist as his mouth came down on hers.

She closed her eyes, enjoying the warmth of his embrace and his sexy, spicy, masculine scent. Even though his mouth claimed hers with intense pressure, he had the softest, most beautifully shaped lips she had ever kissed; the upper one a perfect Cupid's bow, the lower almost too full. *He has a mouth fit for a god.*

The sudden, forbidden passion between them overwhelmed her, not least of all because she had just come from a doomed affair with another man. *You really are hopeless. Helpless too*, she realized. *Done in by the sweetness of his kiss.* His tongue touched her lips, and she opened, tasting the mint of his toothpaste as desire washed over her.

When the endless moment passed, he didn't release her but continued to hold her against his chest. He leaned close to her ear and murmured, "I can't undo the pain you've experienced today. I can't recover those years for you. But I'll do whatever else you want. Anything."

"Anything is a big promise, Victor." She pulled back, admiring the chocolate pools of his eyes. *I could happily drown in them.*

"I mean it," he insisted.

"And if I asked you…" she swallowed hard. "And if I asked you to give me a baby?"

Victor froze, staring thunderstruck into her face for an endless moment. Then he captured her hand in his and guided it down to the front of his jeans. "Feel these?" he murmured, gently wrapping her fingers around his testicles

She swallowed again and nodded, drawing a shaky breath through her nose.

"I'm really fertile. There's a ton of sperm in there. If I thought you would let me, I would put all of it inside you. You could walk out of here pregnant, today." He guided her hand higher, to his painfully swollen erection. "Feel me there? I'm ready to give you what you want right now."

Unable to take in the full scope of his offer, she turned to the details. "How do you know you're fertile?"

"I've donated sperm before. They told me." His tawny cheeks darkened, but he spoke calmly.

"Oh... why?"

He quirked his eyebrow and gave her a wry grin. "I'm shy, Caroline. I wasn't sure I would ever have the opportunity to be a father otherwise."

"Shy, Victor? You don't seem shy to me. You put my hand on your penis and then claim to be timid?"

One corner of his mouth lifted into a wry half-smile. "With you, I'm not. You know me too well. I trust you."

He trusts me. All the reasons why this conversation should end floated away, destroyed by the hot look on his face and the pleasure of his kiss. She couldn't imagine being so deeply, passionately desired. An inferno of lust sizzled through her. His hand slid to her thigh and her control snapped. *I have to have what this man is offering me... right now!* Caroline disengaged her hand from his groin, planted her hands on his shoulders and swung her leg over so she knelt straddling his lap. She wrapped her arms around his neck and laid her lips on his.

Their mouths met with punishing force, each one determined to show the other something... nameless, wordless, but real.

I can hardly believe this happening. This is reckless, her harried conscience shrieked. *Here I am, in my own office, with a former student from my own classes, making out like a teenager.* The very inappropriateness of the situation jangled her overwrought nerves terribly. But for sheer fantasy-fueling naughtiness, one could scarcely imagine a more arousing scenario.

And now, his warm hands slid over the front of her dress, caressing her belly and fondling her breasts tenderly, his fingertips lingering on her sensitive nipples.

Too much fabric muffled the pleasure of his touch, so she unhooked and wriggled out of her bra. Sliding it

9

out from under her dress, she dropped it carelessly behind her.

~

Victor pulled back and stared at the bewitching sight of taut peaks pressing against her bodice. He made an inarticulate sound and leaned forward to taste one, then the other, right through the fabric.

Caroline tilted her head back, giving him greater freedom.

He took it, lifting, shaping and molding her breasts. *How lovely they are, neither large nor small but beautifully round and upright. I want to savor them for hours…*

Footsteps resounded in the hallway as they approached… and passed without pausing.

Reality attempted to break through the drugging embrace. *Not here. This is a terrible place. We should go… somewhere; my apartment, her house, a hotel, the backseat of a car, anywhere.* He tried to force himself to stop touching her so he could make the offer of better privacy, but her hands lifted to the buttons that fastened the front of her dress, opening them and letting the fabric gape, teasing him with a peek at her pretty skin.

His intentions disappeared in a tidal wave of arousal. *One more button and I'll be able to open her dress and see her.*

She released it.

Victor peeled back the fabric to look at her breasts: pale, pale skin, soft as silk, with delicate, rosy nipples hardened to points.

"Victor," she spoke his name softly. Brown eyes met hazel. Her tiny hand curved around one globe and lifted it. "Put that beautiful mouth on me."

It was an invitation he didn't even want to consider resisting. Leaning forward, he kissed the straining tip before opening his mouth on it, sucking gently to pull it in.

~

Caroline moaned. *Victor's mouth is amazing. On my breast, it's even more amazing.*

He tugged and suckled until she squirmed. As her desire grew, the moisture between her thighs gathered until her panties felt damp with it. The erection she had touched through his jeans had felt nice and thick. *I want it inside me,* she thought, and her whole body sizzled in agreement. She reached low, opening his belt, unbuttoning his jeans and pulling down the zipper. It only freed a tiny amount of space, but it sufficed to allow her to slide her hand inside. Through his underwear, she could feel his hardened, pulsing flesh. She gently squeezed.

Victor exhaled sharply. "Oh God, Caroline," he moaned.

She hungered for the feel of his skin, so she backed up and reached into his underwear, touching him intimately. There was no room for vigorous stroking, but her deft fingers caressed him, trailing over the sensitive head.

"More," she urged.

He lifted his mouth back to hers and wriggled his jeans and underwear down to the floor beneath her body. It was an awkward move, but it worked, and it put his hands between her thighs. He cupped her, then ran one finger along the elastic and moved it aside so he could touch her.

She squeezed her eyes shut as Victor's finger explored her. He lovingly traced each fold, dipped once into her vagina and then slid up to her clitoris, where he skillfully caressed and circled until she was panting. Al-

11

ready the tension had nearly reached critical, and his touch came close to putting her in orbit.

"Please, stop," she whispered frantically against his ear.

"Why?"

"If you make me come I'm going to scream."

He chuckled. "I'd like to hear that."

"Not here. Next time, okay?" *There will be a next time. There has to be.*

His slow nod and the brightness in his eyes told her he agreed. "Okay. Where were we?" he asked.

"I was about to take my panties off."

"Good idea."

She could think of no way to stay on him and remove them, so she stood briefly, dropping the scrap of fabric to the floor before she climbed back onto his lap, taking his sex in her hand and stroking once, twice, before positioning him. They arched their hips together and Victor's erection slid through the drenched entrance of Caroline's body.

She exhaled in a whoosh. *I was right. He is a nice size, thick enough to stretch me a little. Just the right length too. The precious delivery will be placed perfectly for maximum effectiveness.* Remembering why they were doing this made the moment even hotter and she moaned softly.

"Oh, Caroline, you're so tight and wet. God, you feel great," he whispered in her ear.

"So do you."

"Ride me, little teacher."

Caroline rose upward, letting Victor's sex glide gloriously inside her. *I'm going to come anyway,* she realized. *I've never been this ready.*

They surged back together, seeking complete penetration again and finding it. The naughtiness of what they were doing, the newness, and the perfect stimulation combined to produce a mutual orgasm of blinding force.

They leaned together and sealed their mouths on each other. They drank in the pleasure noises, keeping each other silent so their passion could remain a secret.

As Caroline returned to awareness, she lowered her head to Victor's shoulder. *I should be embarrassed by what I just did, but I'm not. It was great, the best sex of my life, and I want more of it… more of Victor.*

He lifted her into his arms and lowered her, so she lay on her back on the sofa. Retrieving her panties, he slid them back onto her before pulling up his pants.

She smoothed her dress back down over her legs and he tenderly fastened the buttons.

"Stay there a while," he told her, "let gravity help you."

"Right. Victor?"

He met her eyes. "Yes?"

"That was… wild, but really good."

"It was." He stroked her cheek with his thumb.

"We need to talk. What's next?" *There's something here. There just has to be. And wouldn't such a smart, kind, handsome man be an excellent baby-daddy?*

"Yes, we do. Not here though. Enough is enough. This is going to be a private conversation." He touched his lips to her forehead.

"It is."

"Okay." He brushed her mouth with his again before rising to grab a sticky note and pen from her desk. "Will you please call me?" he begged, his warm brown eyes pleading as he held out the note on which he'd written his number.

Now he turns shy, but it's an easy promise to keep. "Okay, I'll call you tonight. We'll have to find time to get together and talk."

Her promise restored his confidence. "Talk, and other things." He waggled his eyebrows.

"Yes," she said, laughing at his eager expression.

He knelt beside her and kissed her mouth. "I hope you're feeling better."

"Yes. Thank you." She wrapped her arms around his neck for a warm hug. One more quick kiss and he turned and left.

Caroline lay there for several minutes. *Who would have guessed that the shy, handsome student I've always liked so much would suddenly become my lover? Oh, I won't lie. I've always been attracted to him. He's awfully good looking after all; dark and handsome, my favorite, with dark brown hair and medium brown skin.*

Okay, so he isn't particularly tall, but then, I'm so petite it doesn't matter. He's taller than me. I had to struggle so hard to remain professional with him when he came to my office for help, his tee shirt clinging to his sculpted arm and shoulder muscles, his faded jeans riding low on his narrow hips, his sexy cologne filling the room. I'm not quite sure what became of my sense, that I allowed—no, encouraged— him to have sex with me, and here in my office of all places. We were so lucky not to get caught.

What was my motivation? It's complex to be sure. Hmmm.

Her breakup with William, of course, should have meant that she would never have a baby. Desperate longing for a child coupled with her secret attraction to Victor had made sex with him a possibility.

Not to mention I'm just horny. It had been over a month since she and William had been intimate, and even then, their affair had been growing increasingly unsatisfying for the longest time.

Well, I'm satisfied now. A wicked smile crossed her face. *No one will believe this.*

Her mind wandered back to the day that marked the beginning of the end of her previous relationship…

～

The expected knock on the door of her house brought a strange sense of excitement mixed with discomfort. She rose from the sofa and moved in the direction of her formal front entrance—not the side door into the mudroom she and her friends all used.

What does this feeling mean? Since when did my Saturday liaison with my boyfriend cause anxiety? It must have been last week when pinned my arms down... or the week before when he blindfolded me. A cold dread dampening her usual ardor, she twisted the knob and revealed the tall, stately form of her man: dark hair with silver wings, dignified and handsome. His dark eyes burned with an expression that made her deeply uncomfortable.

Should I say something? I don't want to seem like a prude.

He stepped into the room and began to move toward her with a stealthy, predatory step.

She couldn't help but step back. *Apparently, I am a prude, but this game doesn't excite me.* "William, what are you doing?" she demanded, straightening her spine. She set her heels, trying to seem taller.

"Playing chase. It's just a game. God, Carrie, don't you want to have fun in bed? Does it always have to be serious?"

"Please, don't call me Carrie. I've asked you not to, and this doesn't seem like fun to me. You're scaring me. Stop it."

His grin grew even wider until the sight of it made her want to hide. "A little fear can make it even better."

Gulping down her rising panic, she lifted her chin in a show of bravado. "For you, maybe. William, if sex is fun, it's got to be fun for both partners. I don't like what you're doing."

"You don't trust me." He dropped the teasing act and frowned. "You know I would never hurt you, Carrie."

I do know that... or at least I think I do. She tried to

relax and let her boyfriend take her hand. He led her to the bedroom and gently unbuttoning her blouse.

"Undress me, Carrie," he urged. "I know you want this."

She nodded, trying to recapture her rapidly-cooling ardor. *I feel so… wrong*, she thought as he slid her skirt down her thighs, leaving her standing before him in her underwear, feeling more vulnerable and less aroused than she could recall since the relationship began. Determined not to spoil the afternoon, she obediently tugged off his sweater and unbuckled his belt. His pants skimmed down his narrow hips with little prompting.

Caroline shifted on the office couch, not liking the turn her thoughts had taken. She finished the scene quickly in her mind, skimming over the details.

I made a teasing, flippant comment, hoping to restore our shattered comfort level. I can't even remember what I said, but I'll never forget how his dark eyes flashed a second before he put me over his knee and spanked me… hard. God, I hated that. I truly don't understand how pain spurs pleasure in some people, but it clearly doesn't work for me. Four slaps later, and I was still too stunned to react when he dumped me onto the bed and mounted me. I didn't say no. I can't claim it was assault, but it certainly wasn't the kind of sex I enjoy. At least it was over fast. But, damn, that was rough. I was sore for two days afterwards.

And then he started kissing me. That's when I sort of woke up. "Stop it!" *I shoved him away from me, and despite how much bigger he is, I actually moved him enough to escape his crushing weight.*

"What's wrong? That was amazing."

"It was horrible. You hurt me. What's wrong with you?" *I pulled on my underwear so hard I almost tore it. Then I dragged on my bathrobe. Being naked made me feel more vulnerable than ever.*

"It's just a game, Carrie. Kink. What's the matter?"

"Don't call me Carrie," I hissed. I was too angry even to shout. "I. Don't. Like. Kink. Now get out of my house and don't come back."

"Wait, what?" He looked so surprised.

"Are you obtuse? You like it this way, so everyone else must? I told you I was uncomfortable, but you didn't listen. You never listen. You won't even call me by my real name. What kind of boyfriend is that? No, we're through. Get out."

I met his eyes as his expression changed from consternation to awareness to determination.

"Carrie... Caroline... I'm sorry. I didn't realize. It was my mistake. I should have paid closer attention. Please, let's not break up. Give me one more chance. If you don't like kink, I won't do it anymore. I promise."

She had given him one chance, and he'd made the most of it, but it quickly became obvious that the pleasurable vanilla sex she preferred bored him, and the longer they lingered, the less often he was willing to go there with her until it became rare for them to be intimate at all.

That had been months ago. He never complained, but the distance grew with every passing day. *And now it's over. Spectacularly, amazingly over.* The breakup itself had been as tepid as the relationship. No sooner had she said the word 'family' than he'd replied, in a calm, mild voice, that family was not something he intended to have.

That had been the end for her, right there. *I'm glad. I should have ended it ages ago. After all, I'm not what he needs either.*

A noise sounded in the hallway. Emma, the custodian, clattered her bucket of tools over the tile, leaning heavily on her one squeaky shoe.

Caroline, ready to release thoughts of her former

boyfriend, jumped from the couch, grabbed her bra from the corner of her desk where it had been tossed, and stuffed it into her purse just before the customary knock on the door.

"Come in," she called, hoping she looked relatively normal, not like a woman who'd just had amazing, wild sex.

Emma ambled squeakily into the room. "Evenin', Dr. Jones," she said.

"Hello, Emma. How are you doing?"

"Fine, just fine." She scooped up the trash can beside Caroline's desk and dumped the papers and an empty brown bag into her cart.

"Have you heard from your son?" Caroline asked.

Emma smiled. "Yes. He called me yesterday. Says it's hot in Afghanistan." She set the can back on the floor.

"I bet. Is he safe and all?"

Emma's smile faded. "So far."

"And your daughter?"

Emma's frown changed and she beamed. "She had her baby over the weekend. It's a boy."

"Congratulations. What's his name?"

"Darryl James. And thank you. They're just so excited. Would you like to see a picture?"

"Of course!"

Emma reached into her pocket and pulled out her cell phone. A few clicks brought up a picture of a pretty, dark-skinned woman sitting in a hospital bed beside a ghostly pale man with wild red hair and freckles. His arm encircled her. They held a tiny new baby who looked attractively like a mix between the two of them.

"He's going to be a heartbreaker, Emma," Caroline said, smiling.

The custodian grinned even bigger. "How come you don't have any babies, Dr. Jones? You'd be such a nice mother."

Caroline closed her eyes. "I want one, believe me. I hope it's not too late."

The custodian gave her a considering look. "I'll say a prayer for you if you like."

Caroline's eyes burned. "Thank you, Emma. I'll take all the help I can get. Listen, I have to run. Have a good evening."

"See you later, Dr. Jones."

"Caroline, Emma. Please, call me Caroline," she reminded her.

Emma smiled but didn't respond.

Caroline grabbed her purse and coat and hurried into the hallway. *I'm going to be so late meeting my friends, but I have to make a quick stop in the bathroom to put my bra back on.* Pushing through the door, she peeked in the mirror. *Nothing obvious. I look normal.*

She ducked into a stall and quickly hooked herself into the black lace garment. Then she threw on her coat and made her way down the hallway. *No point racing around. I'm already late.* As she descended the stairs, she pulled out her cell phone and dialed Sophie's number.

Her best friend answered.

"Hi, Sophie. It's Caroline. I'm running a little late today."

"Yes, I guess so," her friend replied in a mildly ironic tease. "Are you going to make it?"

"Should I try? I'm almost in the parking lot."

"Yeah, I think we're going to eat here tonight," her friend replied.

Oh, yum! And do I ever have an appetite. "Okay. I'll get there as quick as I can."

"Can we order you something? Your usual?"

Caroline considered her habitual glass of cabernet sauvignon. *It sounds good, but...* "Not tonight. Just order me a raspberry lemonade, please."

"Sure thing. See you in ten."

"If the traffic cooperates."

She had arrived at her car by this time, so she tucked her cell into her purse and clicked the key fob to unlock her car. Her whole body still tingled, and her mind kept replaying the two conversations... with Emma, about babies, with Victor about making one.

This is reckless, foolish, but I can't stop. I want to—no I'm going—to try and make a baby with Victor.

Fifteen minutes later, Caroline arrived at the sports bar where the four women held their usual Monday night get-together.

Inside, the familiar scene seemed to clash with the feeling of newness and unreality currently chewing on her insides. In the central bar area, three huge flat-screen televisions blared a different sport to each side of the room. The fabric upholstering rows of booths along the walls resembled leather, but she suspected it was actually synthetic. The pale wood tables matched the floor. Over each one hung a single-bulb pendant light with a blue stained-glass shade.

She found her friends at their usual booth in the corner and slid into the empty spot by her raspberry lemonade, taking a long sip before greeting everyone. "Hi, sorry I'm late," she said.

Next to Caroline sat Sophie, a small brunette with a friendly smile. "It's okay," Sophie said. "Maggie was just about to tell us her update."

"Yeah, it's a bitch, too," Maggie said, flipping her shoulder-length shin black hair out of her face to reveal her chiseled cheekbones. "My dad just got married again."

"Maggie, you wanted him to. You've always said so," Sophie reminded her.

"Yeah, I did. But, well, not this woman. You all remember my friend Selene, right?"

"Yes, of course," Caroline replied, drawing to mind the image of a kind, quiet woman with white-blond hair. *She looks like a porcelain doll, and yet she's a police in-vestigator. Life is strange like that.*

"Yeah. Her." Maggie sulked.

The other women gasped. "Your dad married her? Isn't she pretty young for him?" Sophie asked.

"Uh-huh. She's only twenty-eight. He just turned forty." A disapproving frown dragged her lips downward, but the theatrical gesture revealed real pain in her dark brown eyes.

"Wow. Twelve years is kind of a lot," Caroline agreed.

"I don't know," Jessie said. Perched on the edge of the bench, she chewed one fingertip and eyed some undergraduates who had turned their attention from the screen to ogle her cleavage. She shifted her shoulders and waggled her eyebrows, pouting decoratively while they wolf-whistled. "An older man can be kind of fun. They know all the moves. I mean, how much older than you is William?"

Caroline blinked. "Nine years, I think."

"See? Twelve isn't that much more than nine."

"It's not the age difference," Sophie suggested, "is it, Maggie? It's that she's your friend."

Maggie exhaled heavily, took a sip of her Heineken, and answered. "Right. I wanted her to find someone. She's alone too much. I guess it's not surprising, since she's had this massive crush on him for years. She would never have gotten together with anyone else, but I didn't realize *he* loved *her* until recently. They moved super fast too. They only got together this summer, and now they're married."

"Well," Caroline said consideringly, "she's really nice, as I recall. Pretty too. I can kind of see it."

"No, I get it," Maggie said fiercely, "and I know I'm going to have to get over it. They're in love, you know, the real deep forever kind. I'm trying to be supportive, but it still bothers the hell out of me."

"Okay," Sophie told her, "It's okay to feel what you feel. Just don't hang on to being mad so long you hurt your relationship with either of them. I know you don't want that."

"You're right." Maggie sighed. "Okay, Caroline's turn. Why were you so late? What happened? You seem a little... flustered."

Caroline took a moment to consider. *Flustered is right.* She didn't want to lie so she told the truth, at least some of it. "I was talking to William. We... broke up."

Sophie lowered her dark eyebrows. "I thought you were going to talk to him about getting married."

Caroline nodded and sipped her drink. "I did. That's why we broke up. He doesn't want to get married, ever. No wife. No kids. I can't live with that. It's a deal-breaker."

"You can't be with someone who isn't going the same direction as you. I'm sorry, Caroline. It's for the best though." Maggie reached across the table and patted her hand.

Caroline smiled a little sadly. *Leave it to plain-spoken Maggie to get straight to the point.*

"No, it's not. William is a great guy!" Jessica interjected. "You're awfully stupid to let him go. Why would you hurt him like that?"

Hurt...him? What a weird thing to say. Trying to understand her friend's perspective instead of reacting to her tactless comment, Caroline protested, "I'm not trying to hurt him, but when two people have completely different priorities in life, how can they work it out?"

Jessica narrowed her eyes. "What about a compromise? You ladies always yack on and on about the right way to do relationships, and how nothing will ever be perfect. You finally have a man, so you should work with what you have. I know he wants you to move in with him."

Her friend's tone drew Caroline's gaze. *What is that look on Jessica's face?* Caroline couldn't read it, but it told her gut something. "So what? It's not the same as being married. Besides, what I really want is a baby, and he's adamant about that. There's not really a compromise possible with such a fundamental difference."

Around the table, the ladies nodded.

Jessica rolled her eyes. "I just don't get it. What's so important about a baby anyway? They're pretty gross."

"That's your opinion, Jessie. Not mine." Caroline narrowed her eyes. "How do you know William wanted me to move in with him? He only said that to me today."

"He told me."

There's that spark again. It almost looks like… excitement. Why would Jessica be excited about this conversation? Caroline crooked one eyebrow and took a guess. "How long have you been sleeping with him?" she asked calmly.

"About a year," Jessica replied, equally calm.

Maggie and Sophie gasped in unison.

How interesting that I don't feel angry or jealous at all. "So that's why he started to lose interest in me. He was busy somewhere else."

Sophie made an uninterpretable sound as though trying to think of something to say.

Jessica shook her head, sending her hair tumbling around her bare shoulders, and cut her off. "He didn't lose interest. He likes you. He thinks you're the perfect woman. He told me. He wants to keep you forever." A hint of bitterness soured her voice as she spoke.

Caroline closed her eyes. *Interesting that after a three-year relationship, Jessie used the word 'like' not love to describe how he felt.* It confirmed Caroline's observations. "He must not know me at all if he thinks I'm going to hang around being his live-in girlfriend while he nails one of my best friends behind my back."

Maggie snorted, an angry sound that promised she

teetered on the brink of unleashing her scary but rarely-aroused temper

Caroline pondered again, prodding the information to see if it provoked a reaction. *Nope. Just as I suspected. Any feeling I may have had is totally dead.* "Jessie, I'm not mad, really. I broke up with him for other reasons. You're welcome to him. Sounds like you two are pretty well suited. Forget about the girlfriends' code. Have at it."

She turned to Sophie and then Maggie, meeting each set of eyes before saying, "Ladies, I don't really feel like eating here tonight. I think I'm going home. See you next week."

Caroline fished a couple of dollars out of her purse for the lemonade and dropped them on the table. She hugged Sophie and Maggie and walked out.

As she headed through the restaurant, she could hear Sophie and Maggie berating Jessica, Jessie answering with snotty insouciance. *I'm glad not to be part of that conversation.*

She picked up a salad from a fast food restaurant before driving through the city to her two-story Victorian home, high on a hill overlooking the lake. Though far from the university—she spent a fortune on gas every month—she had an amazing view. Pulling her car into the generous detached garage, she grabbed her purse and her drive-thru bag and trudged up the gravel drive to her door, letting herself into the mudroom.

Perching on a storage bench to remove her shoes, she hung her coat from a hook on the wall. *Did I leave laundry in the washer? I think I must have.* She peeked in and found a load of wet towels, which she transferred to the dryer, hoping she wouldn't forget to take it out before bed.

Next, she passed into the black granite and stainless-steel kitchen, hanging her keys on a hook at the white pantry cabinet. She didn't feel like sitting politely at the round oak table alone. After such a momentous day, she gave herself permission to be a little slovenly and carried her bag down the hall to the den, where she sprawled on the brown leather sofa.

Television proved to be a flat bore that evening, so she quickly clicked it off and, between bites, rummaged in her purse. Her phone already sat on the coffee table, but she wanted that scrap of paper. *There it is,* she thought with a thrill of triumph as she found it stuck to her checkbook. *Victor Martinez. (612) 732-1584. I have a feeling sleeping with him is going to make getting over William easy. I honestly don't feel sad about the breakup at all, only about the wasted years.*

Her stomach fluttered as she regarded the phone, the paper, and the momentous life changes they represented. Then she firmed her resolve. *Well, I'm not going to waste another moment. I know what I want, and this may be my only chance to get it.* Her salad finished, she tucked the box and the fork back into the bag and dialed the number.

"Hello?"

God, his voice is sexy, so low-pitched, but also soft and gentle. "Victor? It's Caroline."

"Oh, hi. How are you?" he replied, sounding happy.

"I feel sooooo good," she teased in a sultry tone. "You?"

"Great, naturally," he said, and his voice held a hint of masculine satisfaction. Then his typical shyness crept back in. "Any regrets?"

"No, surprisingly not. I've offended my own modesty, but it sure was fun." She giggled. "I wouldn't change a thing."

"Me either," he agreed. "It was a crazy thing to do, though."

"Yes." Caroline wished for a moment her hair was long enough to twine around one finger. She settled for fiddling with the fringed edge of an afghan. "Next time, let's try a bed, okay?"

"So you still want a next time?" he asked, sounding hopeful.

Caroline swallowed down her nervous reaction. *You've already had sex with him. Agreeing to do it again is not nearly as scary.* "I've been thinking about it, and yes, if you're still willing."

"Of course. You know, I didn't offer... what I did on a whim. I'm really attracted to you."

Oh, he's so sweet. His tentative tenderness brings out all kinds of appealing feelings in me. "I realize that, Victor. I've known for a while."

He paused, breathing slowly. She could hear the respiration through the speaker. "So, what we need to work out is exactly what this is. Are we just trying to give you a baby, or is it something more? I'm sure it's no surprise that I vote for the latter."

"It's not a surprise." She sighed. *I wish I had a better answer for him than this.* "I just don't know. I won't lie, I find you really attractive, and I know what a great person you are. I don't want to hurt you, but I've just come from a kind of ugly breakup, as you know. I would hate to get together with you only to find out later that I was just rebounding."

"Honestly, Caroline, I'm willing to risk it," he replied.

Oh wow. "You shouldn't be. You're a wonderful person, Victor. You deserve the best kind of relationship."

"Thank you. But to me, the chance to be with you, even unsettled though everything is, is worth any risk. You mean that much to me."

Her fingers froze on the crocheted fabric. *Not a crush, is it? Tread carefully, Caroline. You don't want to break his heart.* "I'm not sure I'm worth all that," she replied. "Don't put me on a pedestal. I'm just a woman."

"A woman I've been crazy about for years," he reminded her. "Besides, I'm not putting you on a pedestal. We're a little too intimate for that now."

Heat flared in her cheeks. "True."

Another moment of slow, deep breathing resolved into a tentative suggestion. "Okay, I'm sure you need time to think about this, so I have an idea. My extended family owns a cabin outside of Grand Rapids. It's for family reunions, summer vacations, things like that. It's almost Thanksgiving. No one uses it this late in the year. If you don't have huge plans for the holiday, maybe we could go there. It would be a great place to continue... working towards our goal in private. It's also about four hours away, which would give us plenty of time to talk, decide how we want to handle things."

Caroline shivered as the thought of spending time alone with Victor, enjoying their apparently explosive attraction, registered in all its sexy fullness. "That's a good idea. My family is expecting me for Thanksgiving of course, but I don't really like going. My sisters will be there and they both have kids. It's kind of like torture to see all those beautiful babies and not have one of my own, especially since they're both younger than me. I can tell them I have other plans. I doubt anyone will be too put out." She thought for a moment. "You're more fun than Mom's overcooked turkey anyway."

"I'm getting turned on just thinking about it."

"Me too. I can't wait." A naughty grin spread across her face.

"It's a date then. Shall I pick you up Wednesday morning?"

"Sounds good. But, Victor?"

"Yes?"

"Don't come to my office tomorrow," she pleaded.

"Why not?"

"I don't know if I can control myself, and while it was great the one time, I really don't want to get caught with my panties down at work." Her cheeks heated further. *I must look like a tomato.*

Victor laughed. "I understand. I think I can wait one day."

"Good. Have a good night."

"You too." He paused as though he were trying to think of something else to say, before he finally settled on, "Bye."

"Bye, Victor. Sleep well." She hung up. *Thanksgiving is going to be amazing. But what do I want from Victor? I should think that through before Wednesday. It wouldn't be very nice not to have an answer.* While she was debating the relative merits of the different options, her phone rang. Thinking it might be him, she picked up quickly.

"Hello?"

"Carrie?" The false dignity in William's voice sounded oily and obnoxious in light of all the new revelations she'd had.

"Don't call me Carrie!" she snapped. "You know I don't like it. In fact, why are you calling me at all? I asked you not to."

"I can't help it. I don't want to break up."

Why on earth would a mature, sophisticated man speak in such a whining tone? Disgusted, Caroline replied bluntly, "It's done, William."

"Please reconsider. We had such a great relationship."

She snorted. "You must be out of your mind. It was not great at all. You stopped wanting me a long time ago, you have no idea who I am or what I want in life and you don't even care, and you're sleeping with my friend. What part of that is supposed to tempt me?"

William sighed. "I asked Jessie to keep her mouth shut."

Caroline rolled her eyes. "I figured it out. If you want to be with her, be with her. Leave me the hell alone."

"I don't want to be with her," William protested, a hint of that whine creeping back into his voice. "She's a fun girl, but not really someone I want to introduce to my colleagues, bring home for the holidays."

Caroline shook her head. *That doesn't make any sense.* "Are you saying you want me to be your... what? I don't understand."

"Caroline, you're beautiful, intelligent, and articulate. Everyone who meets you loves you. My colleagues are very impressed. My parents are crazy about you."

A month ago that would have moved me to tears. Today it just feels like manipulation, not to mention that he whines like a ditzy freshman cheerleader. "It sounds like everyone likes me except you," she drawled.

"No, seriously. I want you to move in with me. If it means so much to you, I guess we could get... engaged."

Caroline placed her free hand over her face. *For an intelligent man, he sure is slow to understand the simplest things.* "Engaged, but never married? And would we be monogamous? Would you give me a baby?"

Silence.

"No, thank you. Listen, we both know you prefer a wild girl, and you have one. Just be honest with yourself about it. I'm not even a little bit interested in being your pseudo-Stepford wife, and covering for the fact that you want something... dirtier."

"Why not?" he drawled, finally showing a hint of anger. "It's not as though you actually like sex anyway."

Caroline blinked in surprise. "What on earth gave you that idea?"

"You did. Am I wrong?"

Victor was right to call him a jackass. Rolling her eyes, Caroline studied the warm honey-colored beams spanning her ceiling as she silently counted to five. *Nope, not going to work.* "Actually, no. I haven't liked sex for a while... with you," she said bluntly. "It was pretty boring. Now, my new lover… he's great. I think I'll keep him. You, however, are through. Find someone else, if having a cover for your tendencies is so important to you, but please be honest with her about what you want. I wasted three years of my life on you, and I'm not getting any younger. Goodbye, William. Don't call me again."

She hung up.

The phone rang immediately but a quick check of the screen revealed the familiar number and she ignored it. He kept calling with such persistence, she finally turned off the phone altogether, abandoning it in the kitchen when she went to throw away her trash. Then she gathered up a warm armload of purple towels and slowly climbed the stairs to her bedroom.

She dumped the clean, fragrant pile on her bed and folded quickly, delivering them to the linen closet before brushing her teeth in the white scalloped pedestal sink. As she spat toothpaste, she looked at the wallpaper: black with pink roses. *Dated to the extreme. It looks like the 1980s threw up in here. Renovating this bathroom is going to be my summer project.*

"Wait?" she asked aloud, realization dawning. "Am I going to have time for a summer project? If I manage to get pregnant, I'll be having a baby right at that time." The thought shook her. "I can't worry about that right now. Not yet."

She flipped off the lights and trudged down the creaky floorboards of the hallway back to her bedroom, where she changed into a flannel nightgown, pulled down her violet and lace comforter, and snuggled into her cozy bed.

Sleep did not find her easily.

CHAPTER 2

The weather on Wednesday morning didn't look too promising. The lake, almost frozen enough to stand on, reflected a sky the color of gunmetal. Already denuded completely of their colorful foliage, tree branches clawed the sky with gnarled fingers.

Caroline clung tight to her coffee cup, trying to keep her hands warm while she waited for Victor to pick her up. Her belly thrilled over and over with nervous excitement. *Spending the long weekend snuggled in bed with him sounds incredibly appealing. Much better than another holiday with the family.*

She rolled her eyes. *At least my sisters understood when I told them it's just too hard to see their children when I don't know if I'll ever have my own.*

Her mother had complained about her breakup with William, whom she liked very much. *Another good reason to stay away. The last thing I want is to listen to more lectures.*

She didn't feel ready to tell anyone about her new lover. A naughty grin curved her lips. *I want to keep him to myself for a while, savor him in secret.*

A knock sounded on the door. Bracing herself, she took a deep breath, her heart pounding against the inside of her rib cage with the force of a sledgehammer.

Gulping, she opened and found herself looking into warm brown eyes. She pulled him inside and quickly shut the door. Setting her cup on the bench, she slid her arms around his neck.

He lowered his mouth, treating her to a long, wet kiss.

The moment Victor's lips touched hers, Caroline went up in flames. As hot as their forbidden liaison in her office had been, today, desire burned hotter.

Yes! The little voice inside her cheered. *He's every bit as delicious as I remember. I had so feared the desire between us was a onetime event, due to the unusual circumstances.*

It wasn't.

They lingered, mouth to mouth, neither willing to pull away as pleasurable tension built within them. They opened together, tongues tangling lustily as Victor's strong arms wrapped around her waist. His hands cupped her bottom and pressed her pelvis to his.

At last, they pulled back, panting, stunned at the volcanic arousal each generated in the other.

"Wow," Victor breathed, "that was even better than I remember. If we don't stop, we might as well just stay here a while. I'll never be able to drive. Caroline, you're amazing."

"I can't imagine such intensity," she replied, just as stunned as he seemed. "I was attracted to you when you were a freshman, but I had no idea us being together would be like this. Um," she pressed her hand to his cheek, "you're kind of cold. I have some coffee if you want a cup."

"Yes, that would be nice. I don't think I'll be able to sit in the car for a few minutes anyway." He pressed uncomfortably against his straining erection.

Caroline grinned. "I can't wait to get familiar with that again."

"Please, don't talk about it," he begged. "I need to think about something else or I'm going to have to have

32

you right here before we leave." He leveled a lustful look at her.

"Oh, sorry," she said with an unrepentant grin. "Let me get you that coffee. Or here, come with me."

Sliding her hand into his, she scooped up her own cup and led him from the mudroom into the kitchen. Opening the cabinet to the left of the sink, she pulled out a mug with a sketch of William Shakespeare on it and filled it with coffee, handing it to Victor "Milk or sugar?" she asked, reaching for the handle of the refrigerator.

"Black is fine," he replied.

He raised it to his mouth, leaning his hip against the granite, his eyes far away. "I remember this cup. You used to sip coffee from it in class and I would think how lucky this guy was to be so close to your pretty lips. It's pathetic to be jealous of a mug, isn't it?" He covered his blush with a deep gulp of the coffee and an appreciative sigh.

"Wow, you did have it bad, didn't you?" she teased gently.

His eyes turned intense. He pushed up from the counter and crossed to stand beside her. "Not much has changed."

"Except now you're closer to me than that cup." She stroked her fingers down his chest.

"Right. I've tasted more than your lips." He slid his arm around her. "Damn it, I asked you to stop, but I'm just as bad."

Propriety and embarrassment warred within her. She bit her lip. "Victor," she leaned her forehead against his chest, "I have to tell you something, and it's probably going to take the wind right out of your sails."

"What's that?"

She paused a moment, wondering what words to use. "Okay, I know it's bad etiquette to talk to your new lover about the old one, but this affects you. I found out

33

something really... not good. I told you about William. He and I have been... intimate for the last two years. When you and I were together in my office, I didn't worry about that because I assumed he and I had been monogamous. That there would be no risk to you." She swallowed hard, biting her lip again. *Damn, this feels horrible.*

Shuddering, she made herself continue. "That's not the case. I found out that he's been sleeping with someone else for the last year. I hate to say it, it's so embarrassing, but I have no idea what I've been exposed to. I went to the doctor yesterday and got a battery of tests just to be sure, but the results haven't come in yet." Caroline sighed.

Victor's face twisted into revolted sympathy. "I'm sorry. I have to tell you, he sounds like a loser."

Caroline's lip trembled. "I'm starting to agree. It kills me that I wasted three years of my life on him."

He trailed his fingers down her cheek. "It's done. Don't keep on wasting time by regretting it. Okay, to continue the awkward conversation, what level of exposure are we talking about here? You and I are deliberately having unprotected sex, so I guess I need to know if you two did. After two years, a lot of couples forget about condoms and use something else."

Did I ever trust him enough for that? "No, it was condoms, every time."

"Well, that's good. Was he... promiscuous?"

She shook her head. "No. He's been sleeping with my friend Jessica. The thing is, *she* is... Well, she's just kind of a slut." *Rude to say, but at this point, I'm entitled to be less than polite.* "That's where the risk comes from. I have no idea what she's been up to, if she's careful, anything. It's scary. I used to think that no man in his right mind would go to bed with someone like her. Now, in a real sense, I have." Caroline shuddered.

Victor gripped shook his head in disbelief. "He was

with your friend? Oh God. How did you get mixed up with this guy? And what on earth is wrong with your friend?"

She shrugged. "It's just the way she is," Caroline replied with a shrug. "I'm not surprised, so I guess maybe I'm just stupid. Not least of all because my relationship with William hasn't been good in a while. It was kind of nice at first, but then, for the last year, it's been going downhill. If there's a bright spot in the situation, it's that he seems to have lost interest in me, and our... intimate moments have been very few and far between. It was a month before you and I got together, and before that, six weeks."

Victor nodded. "Sounds like it's been waning for a while."

"Yes, basically for the last year. Now that I know about Jessica, it makes sense, but *why* didn't I just break things off?" *And why are you whining, Caroline?* She cut off the flow of words, shutting her mouth with a snap.

"I can guess why," he told her, smoothing a strand of short, dark hair off her forehead. "You seem like a cautious woman, one who doesn't risk her heart or body easily. I suppose, having committed to that relationship, you were reluctant to admit it had been a mistake. That's what it was Caroline—a mistake. You're not stupid. You're still a good girl."

"Yes," she said ironically, "a good girl who has sex with her student in her unlocked office."

"Well, maybe you do have a wild streak." He smirked at her. "That might be fun. Do you?" He stepped forward, placing himself firmly in her personal space, so his scent wafted over her.

"I... I don't know." Her eyes skated away and her shoulders tensed, though she made no move to step back.

He placed one hand against her hip, and even through jeans and a sweater, she would have sworn she could feel the warmth of the touch on her skin. At the same time, he gave her cryptic response another funny look.

She shook her head. "I've confessed enough for right now. That doesn't affect us. Anyway, the question at hand is, knowing that I've been exposed to who knows what, are you willing to risk your own health by continuing this?"

"Let me think." Victor tapped his thumb against his front teeth and began gnawing on the nail. "Okay, the risk is real, but you say you weren't with him much in the last year, during the time he was sleeping with your friend. You also say you used condoms with him. Most likely, if you were going to… get sick, you would have had some kind of symptoms. I think they mostly show up in the first month. Have you noticed anything?"

She blushed. "No, and I've been pondering, believe me, but the big scary ones don't have symptoms for years." Even the oblique reference made her stomach clench.

He set the cup down, wrapped his arm back around her and gave her a little squeeze. "Right. But still, I think you've managed to minimize your own exposure. Besides, we've already done it once. Does it really make a big difference if we continue?"

She put her hands on his shoulders and looked up into his eyes. "I don't know. I don't want to stop. You're kind of habit-forming, Victor." His eyes turned to chocolate fire. "But I also don't want to put you in any danger."

He smiled. "Thank you. No, I don't want to stop either. I guess I can just risk it."

"Are you sure?"

He chuckled. "When you stand there looking all pretty, and I think that I get to take you away to a private place and play with you for five days? Yes, I'm sure."

She nodded, thankful to have the serious conversation done so they could continue with the fun and teasing. Her coffee gone, she rinsed out the cup and left it in the dish drainer. He gulped his and followed suit.

"Shall we get going?" he suggested.

Warmth suffused her, despite the chilly edge even the central heating in her house couldn't dispel. "Okay. *I'm ready, let's go." She turned back toward the door.*

"Do you have any luggage?"

Oh yeah. Clothes. Toothbrush. Wake up, Caroline. Stop thinking with your vagina. "Just a small suitcase. It's in my room. Follow me." She took his hand.

"To your bedroom?" Victor's eyes widened.

"Sure. We're going away this weekend, but don't you think you'll be in there with me, later on?"

"I'm hoping." He winked at her and she laughed.

~

Caroline led the way into her room.

Victor stopped to take a good look at her queen-sized bed. *It's certainly big enough for the two of us when the time comes to sleep over.* He could tolerate the lace and satin if he got to touch her underneath it.

The white wicker rocking chair and matching hope chest were a little much for his taste, though. As was the antique dresser with the huge oval mirror mounted above it… *Wait. Mirror? That might not be so bad after all.*

She scooped up a suitcase from the foot of the bed.

"I would love to kiss you right now," he told her, the heat of his desire bleeding into his voice when he imagined her lying on the bed, thighs parted, waiting to receive him.

"You'd better not, or we'll never get going," she countered, clearly able to see the direction his thoughts had taken.

Victor dug his nails into the palms of his hands. The

sting sufficed to distract him from his growing arousal. "Right. Besides, we still have a few more things to discuss, and I would really like to get it done before we get intimate again."

"Yes," she agreed, tugging on his arm, "Let's go."

They walked, hand in hand, back down to the mudroom, where Caroline bundled up in her coat, hat and gloves and sat on the bench to slide on her boots. "Victor, am I going to need shoes other than snow boots this trip?"

He thought for a minute. "Probably just some slippers. I imagine the cabin floor is pretty cold."

"Oh, I have those." She waved one hand at the suitcase, which she'd placed on the bench.

"Then I think you should be set."

They stepped out into the biting cold and Caroline locked the door. Immediately, her boots lost traction on the icy sidewalk.

Victor wrapped his arm around her waist to steady her as they made their way to his battered black Suburban. *Even though I can't feel her warmth through her puffer coat, it's still nice to hold her.* He opened the back and she tossed her suitcase in, and then he opened the car door for her, taking her hand so she could climb into the seat. Her hazel eyes darkened, and she tugged him down for a sweet, soft kiss on the lips.

Entranced, as always, by the sensation of Caroline's kiss—not to mention her obvious attraction—Victor lost track of time until a teasing blast of icy wind distracted the couple and sent them shivering into the vehicle, doors shut and heater blasting.

As they backed out of her driveway, turning left and heading towards the Interstate, Caroline decided there was no point in waiting. *Best to get this tough conversation*

out of the way first off. "Okay, Victor, I've been doing a lot of thinking. First of all, are you still settled in your mind about what you want?"

"I am," he replied.

It pleased her to note his sexy teasing had been replaced with the serious, thoughtful tone she remembered from class. Smiling, she continued. "And just to be clear, what you're asking is to be my boyfriend while we try to make a baby together."

He glanced at her and nodded. "Yes, and afterwards. I can't imagine losing interest in you. Ideally, I would love this to be as normal a relationship as possible, the kind where both people feel that it at least has the potential to become... permanent." He swallowed hard. "And just so you know, Caroline, I do believe in marriage."

Her grin widened. "I'm glad to hear it. Okay, that's kind of what I thought. I've been thinking about this, and..." she bit her lip, "it seems like a good idea."

Victor exhaled in obvious relief.

She rushed on. "I can't imagine myself sleeping with someone who isn't my boyfriend. That's not my way, despite any evidence to the contrary. Besides, if we... succeed, it's best for a child to have two parents and have them be together. I never did want the life of a single mother; it was a last resort. I suspect I'll prefer to have your support. If this can be worked out, it would be best for all of us."

Victor nodded, concentrating on the road, but she could see by him paying close attention to her words.

She continued, striving for honesty. "I'm still concerned this... wild attraction I feel for you might be rooted in other things, and I really don't want to hurt you, but I do believe there may be a certain amount of choice on my part. You're a good man, and I know a lot about you from the time you were in my class. I know objectively that you have the kind of qualities I want in

39

a long term... or permanent partner. I think, if there should be any awkwardness down the road, I would just be able to deal with it. That's always part of a relationship. And I was attracted to you when you were my student, I just didn't let myself act on it, and that was before I got together with William, so at least some of it is intrinsic to me, to us."

"It sounds like you know what you want as well," he said, turning hopeful eyes her direction for a moment before returning to the road.

"I do. But there's one thing I have to know before I say yes."

"What's that?"

Caroline made a face, fixing her gaze on Victor's profile. "How old are you? You're a senior at the university. That usually implies a certain youthfulness. I can't tell by looking, but there's no way I can conceive of being with a twenty-one-year-old man. You know how old I am. I realize you're probably younger than me, but how much? Please say it's not twelve years."

He didn't turn, but he did smile. Grooves she had never noticed before bracketed his mouth while the corners of his eyes crinkled. "I'm a little younger than you, but not as much as you might think. I'm not twenty-one. Actually, my thirty-first birthday is in December."

She raised her eyebrows. "Thirty-one? Are you serious? Only two years?"

"Yes. I did a four-year stint in the Army after high school, and then I still didn't know what I wanted to do, so I worked with my dad in his shop for six years while I thought about it."

A whoosh of air escaped from between her lips. "Oh. Well, that's fine then. So, Victor, would you like to be my boyfriend?"

The crinkles deepened. "Oh yes, Caroline. I would like that very much."

She laughed in relief. "Good. I still feel a little funny

about having sex with you when we've just gotten to-gether, but it's better than doing it when we're not together."

"I agree. Good. Wonderful." He raised her gloved hand to his mouth, kissing it gently.

She stroked his cheek.

"So, little teacher," Victor continued, "I know you as a professor and a little bit as a lover, but I would like to know you as my girlfriend. What are some things about you I should know?"

"What kind of things?" she asked to quell the flood of incomprehensible gibberish his question elicited in her mind.

"Mundane things."

"Hmmm." She looked out the window. The gray sky hadn't relented. If anything, the heavy clouds hung lower. The fields they passed contained nothing but stubby dry stalks poking above slushy, half-frozen mud. She blurted out the first idea that came to mind. "I hate being called Carrie."

"Noted," he replied, and his serious tone implied no mockery.

Good. I've had to answer too many questions about my name already. Unauthorized nicknames are neither fun nor cute. "What about you?" she prompted.

"I'm half Mexican." He didn't look at her, just sig-naled he was changing lanes and passed a slow-moving minivan full of pre-teens making faces in the window.

"I figured that out," she told him. "Well, not neces-sarily Mexican, but I knew you were Hispanic. I mean, your last name is Martinez. Besides, with those beau-tiful brown eyes, what else could you be?"

His cheeks colored at the compliment. "My dad was born in Guadalajara. He moved to the U.S. when he was eight. It doesn't bother you, does it?" He glanced at her.

She quirked an eyebrow at him in response.

"Never mind. Obviously not."

"Not a bit. Okay..." she thought a minute. *Make it like a writing exercise, Caroline. What can you come up with in ten seconds or less?* "My favorite drink is red wine, but sometimes I like it in a sangria. You?"

"Corona is good, but I'm not opposed to whatever. Except I don't like Schnapps."

"Good to know." She paused. "I have two sisters and my parents are divorced."

"I'm an only child. My parents are a couple but they've never married."

"Why not?" she blurted before realizing it was an impertinent question.

"Mom's kind of a hippie," Victor explained. "You would have to know her. She and Dad love each other, but she believes that marriage is pointless. I don't agree, but that's their business."

"Interesting. I would like to meet them someday," she commented. *Duh, that's what people do in relationships.* Then her heart sank as she imagined Victor meeting her mother.

He grinned, not noticing her momentary lapse in good cheer. "We'll work on that soon. Anything else?"

"I'm allergic to ragweed."

Victor laughed at her lame comment. "Who isn't?"

Now well immersed in the back-and-forth conversation, the next words tumbled out of Caroline's mouth before she could stop them. "I don't like kinky sex." Her cheeks burned at the blunt admission.

Victor paused to consider. The road wound sharply to the right past an abandoned farm. "Hmmm. That could mean a lot of different things. Could you please elaborate? I don't want to kill the moment by accident."

She shook her head, cheeks burning in embarrassment. "It shouldn't come up unless there are things about you I don't know. I don't think I'm a prude."

"No, there's a good bit of evidence to the contrary." He reached over and squeezed her hand. "Granted, I don't have much to go on, but you seemed pretty hot and willing."

"Yes, but that was just nice lovemaking," she protested.

"In an almost public place," he reminded her.

"Okay, so I lost control a little," Caroline admitted, knowing the heat in her cheeks had nothing to do with windburn. "You're hard to resist. You always were. This time it was worse. But it was you, it wasn't the office."

He squeezed her fingers, which she took to be an acknowledgment. "So then, what do you mean by kinky?"

"Well…" her face felt like an inferno, but she forced out, "I don't want to be tied up or spanked. Mixing pleasure with pain doesn't do anything for me."

His expression turned knowing. "Ah, that kind. Well, I don't think you'll need to worry about it. I don't really like to play that way either."

"You've tried it?" Her eyebrows shot toward her hairline. *Shy Victor has tried kink?*

"Yes." Victor's skin turned faintly pink. "I had a relationship when I was in the Army. There was this girl who thought it was her mission in life to find shy boys and… initiate them. She would do pretty much anything. So because of her, I know a great deal about what I do and don't like."

"Ah. Wild girls again. What is it about them?" Caroline wondered aloud, only half joking.

"They're easy." Victor's eyes slid her direction as he stated the obvious.

"Isn't that a bad thing?" Caroline demanded.

Victor shrugged. "Yes. I regret that relationship now that I'm older. At twenty it made sense."

Caroline snorted. "Oh, the stupid things we do when we're young. So what happened?"

"I didn't really understand that it was always meant to be temporary. I asked her to marry me. She refused.

43

She said I was getting too attached and broke things off."

"I'm sorry." This time she squeezed his hand reassuringly.

Victor pursed his lips. "So was I. I was pretty gun shy after that for a long time."

"Until now?" she guessed.

"Uh-huh."

"So only one then? That fits."

"Yup. I bet you're the same, aren't you?"

"Almost."

He waited, but she didn't elaborate, choosing instead to look out the window.

"Oh come on, Caroline. Just what did you do that was so embarrassing?"

"I've only told one person about this," she protested, cheeks burning. "Why would I tell you?"

"In the interests of honesty," he replied. "I think, after all you've just been through, you're probably craving a transparent relationship, one where everything is clearly laid out. I'm okay with that, but it needs to go both ways. You already know more about me than I do about you."

She sighed. "Fine. Maybe I'm not as good a girl as you think."

His breath exhaled in what almost sounded like a disbelieving snort. "I would be very surprised."

"You will be," she retorted, dryly.

"Tell me, Caroline. Let it out."

She went silent, considering, watching as they drove past a frozen pond with icy cattails clustered on the bank. "It all starts with my friend Jessica."

"The one who's sleeping with your ex-boyfriend?" Victor interrupted.

"Yes."

"Sounds like you need better friends."

"Just that one," Caroline acknowledged. "My other friends are great."

"Okay, what happened?" he asked, urging her to get to the point.

Caroline frowned, disliking the memory. "We've known each other forever. We went to the same high school, and then to the same college, not on purpose, though. It was just a coincidence, but since we knew each other, we kind of hung out together."

Caroline shook her head. "So, she thought I was too boring, studying all the time, and she took me to a really wild party. Drinking, drugs, everything. I had never seen anything like it." She turned to Victor and saw a little pair of vertical lines form between his eyebrows. *He's taking it in*, Caroline thought as she continued.

"She handed me a drink. I'd never had alcohol before and it went to my head pretty fast. I don't know exactly how much I drank that night. Too much, for sure. I started losing my grip on consciousness. You know that place where you're semi-coherent, slightly aware but not really awake?"

"Sort of." The downward twist of his gorgeous lips showed he didn't like where this was headed.

"Well, I have these flashes of memory. There was a man. Tall. Blond hair. Built like an athlete. If he told me his name, I have no idea what it was. I remember saying yes. Then I don't remember anything else until the next morning."

Victor's eyebrows drew together. The skin of his cheek sucked inward, making his cheekbone look even more prominent. "Are you sure it actually happened? An intelligent man will realize a half passed out girl can't give consent. He may have stopped."

"No." She swallowed against a burn in her throat and forced herself to speak in a flat, neutral tone. "When I woke up I had blood in my underwear, and I was really sore." She paused, cleared her throat and

45

continued. "What kind of person gives up her virginity in a one night stand and can't even remember it?"

Victor squeezed her hand again. His voice when he answered had turned kind. "An unfortunate one. I'm so sorry that happened to you. Where boys, girls and alcohol mix, consent goes out the window. The law even acknowledges that you were responsible. You know that, right? Your only mistake was to show up. Shame on your friend for taking you there." More than a hint of anger mixed into his sympathetic tone.

"Shame on me for not leaving immediately," she shot back, not ready to relinquish responsibility for her role in the disaster. "I was nineteen, old enough not to succumb to peer pressure. The worst part was after. My college was full of tall blonds. It was terrible to look at them and wonder which one had had me and if he remembered it. Thankfully the worst consequence of that binge was the embarrassment. I didn't get pregnant or sick, and at least I learned one lesson from the experience. I never got drunk again. In fact, it was years before I would even allow myself a glass of wine. I didn't like the way I behaved when I was under the influence."

Victor's lips twisted. "If your intention is to prove that you're some kind of slut, it won't work. I don't think that exactly counts. Even if you said yes, you didn't know what you were doing, which makes it a crime, not a sexual choice. Other than that, you're thirty-three with a single long-term relationship in the past, plus one new one. That's nothing. You're pretty innocent, I think."

She smiled sadly. "Thank you, Victor. I wasn't trying to make you think I'm a slut. It's just that I kind of feel like one. Especially with this situation." She gestured to their joined hands. "I never imagined I would be capable of changing partners so quickly."

"It's the baby thing," he hastened to reassure her. "If

46

you weren't facing your last chance at motherhood, what would you be doing?"

"I don't know. Crying?" she suggested. "This is more fun than crying." She rubbed his thumb with hers. "I'm not sure if I would ever have gotten with you if you hadn't happened to stop in at just that moment. Maybe it's fate."

"Maybe it is," he agreed, grinning. "Were you really that attracted to me when I was in your class? I never noticed it."

She reached across the cab and stroked his cheek. The rough stubble snagged in the strands of her glove. "Yes, I was. Sometimes it was all I could do to hang on to my professionalism. You attracted me so much, it seriously strained my good intentions."

His grin widened, showing white, straight teeth. "I like the sound of that. So, are you ready to go be unprofessional for the rest of the week?"

Unable to suppress a giggle, she replied, "I can hardly wait."

They drove along, continuing their conversation, getting to know each other on a personal level, trying to be casual so the overwhelming desire between them didn't get out of hand ahead of time.

Eventually, the interstate gave way to county roads, and then Victor turned onto a long gravel path, which ended at a gigantic white pine. Tucked beneath its fragrant branches nestled a little jewel of a cabin of rough-hewn logs with a red stone chimney.

"Well, this is it." Victor's voice sounded tense, which matched Caroline's pounding heart.

"Suddenly I can't believe we're really doing this," she said softly.

"I know, but we are. Shall we go inside?" He indicated the structure with one hand.

"Yes. Quickly, please. It's freezing out here."

"The cabin hasn't been used since September," he

pointed out. "I doubt it's warmer inside, at least not until I get the fire going."

"You know how to make fires?" she asked, impressed. "I only know how to make a fire with a gas log and a remote control."

He pulled a teasingly smug, self-satisfied face. "Yes. I was a Boy Scout before I was a soldier. I know how to make fires, even in fireplaces."

"Good."

They struggled out of the car, cursing at the biting wind, and Caroline collected her suitcase while Victor pulled his own luggage out of the trunk. He had a backpack and a grocery bag, but also a big plastic box.

"What's that?" she asked through chattering teeth. Her hunched shoulders had already begun to ache.

"Bedding. There are mice. We can't leave fabric here over the winter."

"Mice? Ew!"

He chuckled. "Yep. I can remember during many summer visits seeing my Tia Lupita chasing them with a broom and cussing them in Spanish. That woman would put sailors to shame... when she's not praying the Rosary."

Caroline giggled until a frozen gust stole her breath.

"Caroline, can you please get the key out of my pocket?" Victor suggested. "My hands are full."

"Sure. Which pocket?"

"My jacket."

Sliding her trembling hand inside, she felt the heat of his body. She gave herself a second to enjoy it before pulling out the key and hurrying to unlock the door.

His prediction proved right. The interior of the cabin felt just as cold as outside, except that the walls did block the wind. Stepping away from the drafty doorway, she took in the building. A large central room contained a fireplace on one end, surrounded by comfortable sofas and recliners. On the opposite wall, under the balcony, resided a kitchen with a gas stove and a stainless steel sink. On the far side from the entrance were two open doors; one to a small bedroom, the other to a bathroom. In the loft area, she saw three more bedrooms filled with bunk beds. For its small size, this cabin appeared to sleep a large number of people.

"What a cute place," Caroline commented. Though she could still feel the cold down deep into her bones, the blocking of the wind had sufficed to stop her painful shivering.

"Thanks. I've always liked it here," Victor replied. "Okay, I'm going to get the fire started."

"I'll make up the bed, okay? Where do you want to sleep? How many bedrooms are there?"

"Four," he replied, setting the grocery bag on the table and moving across the room to collect firewood from a brass bin on the hearth. "But three are upstairs. I don't think it's going to be feasible to go there. The only heat comes from the fireplace. We never come here in the winter."

She scanned the room again. "Well, the downstairs bedroom is pretty close to the fireplace."

"It is." He stacked the logs in the fireplace and began adding crumpled newspaper, "and we can certainly sleep in there if you want. I think it will be warm enough, except..."

"Except what?"

"That's where my *abuela* sleeps."

"Your grandmother?" she asked, glad she remembered a little from her undergraduate Spanish classes.

"Yes."

She winced. "I see your point. I don't particularly want to have sex in your grandmother's bed. What option does that leave us?"

He eyed the sitting area. "This sofa is a pull out bed. I've slept on it before and found it... comfortable. Can we try it?"

"Sure."

"Sounds good." Victor began messing with the flue.

Caroline lifted the red plaid cushions off the sofa, praying there wasn't a nest of rodents inside, and pulled out the internal mechanism that transformed it into a bed. Unfolding it, she examined the mattress. Some wise person had zipped it into a plastic sheet to deter vermin. It looked nicer than the ones that usually came with that type of furniture; thick and—when she pressed on it—soft.

Pulling off the mattress protector, she removed a set of flannel sheets from the box Victor had brought. As she quickly placed the bedding on the bed, her hands were starting to shake from the cold, even with her gloves on. *Fireplace fires always take such a long time to get going.* She quickly added the two heavy blankets and the down comforter.

Now the pull-out bed began to look cozily inviting. She had to test it out. Trudging to the door, she abandoned her boots and coat and shivered as she made her way back across the icy wood floor to the bed, where she quickly slipped under the covers. *What a shame my body heat isn't sufficient to warm me completely, even with all these blankets.* Thankfully, the mattress cradled her in perfect, body-hugging comfort.

She felt it dip as Victor joined her. He pulled her close to him. "How clever you are, little teacher," he told her tenderly.

"Why is that?" she asked, unable to think, distracted by the magnetic lure of his luscious, thick-lashed eyes.

"To combine all the best ideas in one," he explained. "We can warm each other while we wait for the fire to do its thing."

"Yes. I'm so cold, Victor," she complained, pouting like a child.

"Me too. Shall we snuggle? That's a good way to keep warm."

"Oh yes." *This is just as fantasy-fueling as our previous encounter but in a completely different way.* Caroline enjoyed the powerful romance of being cuddled up in front of a fire in a cabin in the woods in the winter.

They aligned their bodies, arms around each other. By mutual consent, they moved towards each other for a kiss. Caroline just couldn't get enough of Victor's mouth. It felt so good on hers.

He opened, tasting her. The tip of his tongue slid between her lips and then pressed deeper, opening her mouth.

She lay passive, making him take the lead.

He licked and caressed the inside of her mouth, teasing her tongue with his. Then he pulled back. "Is something wrong?"

"No, why?" she asked languidly.

"You're not responding." His dark eyes filled with concern

"I'm enjoying," she replied, her voice slurred, drunk on their rising pleasure.

"Oh." He kissed her again, deeply.

"Victor?" she said, reluctantly dragging her lips from his.

"Yes?"

"I have a confession."

"What's that?"

She traced his lips with one fingertip. "I think I'm in love with your mouth. I've been lusting after it since you kissed me in my office the other day. I want it all over me."

His voice grew hot and his dark eyes burned. "You can count on that. I can't imagine a part of your body I wouldn't love to taste, once we warm up a little."

"Good. I'm feeling warmer already."

Oddly, after their rush to get to the cabin, neither one felt any great hurry to get to it. The kissing alone lasted ages. After a while, Caroline began to respond, teasing Victor's mouth and then taking his plump lower lip between her teeth and nibbling it gently.

As the warmth from the fire spread through the room, they began to shed layers of clothing, starting with Caroline's gloves. Victor peeled one and then the other from her hands and tasted each fingertip, biting them so gently as he scraped his teeth over the sensitive skin.

Caroline gasped. She had never imagined her hands could be erogenous zones, but apparently, they were.

Victor kissed her palm and tongued it. Then he placed her two hands on the back of his neck so he could kiss her mouth again.

"Victor?"

"Hmmm?"

"I'm not cold anymore. Would you please help me take my sweater off?"

"Oh yes." His hands slid against her skin, not exactly warm, but not freezing either. He skimmed them over her sides as he lifted the garment off her body.

"How pretty you are, Caroline," he told her as he looked at her almost bare torso, "Show me the rest."

She reached behind her and unhooked her bra, removing it slowly.

As her delicate breasts became visible, Victor drew in an unsteady breath. "Perfect." He placed one hand on each globe, holding them for a long moment before he began to caress and massage them. Her nipples rose eagerly against his palms and he leaned down and suckled first one and then the other.

"Oh yes," she sighed, "That feels wonderful. I'm getting so wet, Victor."

"Are you? That's good."

He sucked and nibbled her until each breath she drew released in a moan of pleasure. Then he pulled off his own sweater.

She shifted, rubbing her nipples on his skin, and he growled.

"I have to get out of these jeans," he told her.

She stroked her way down his body to release the button and zipper before turning to her own. Removing denim while lying on flannel proved frustrating, so she dared to slip out from under the covers as she stripped herself bare. The room had grown significantly more comfortable, even on her bare skin. She knelt on the bed, completely nude, enjoying the warmth of the fire.

"Oh, Caroline, look at you." Victor's voice was sweet and slow as honey. "You look ethereal. A tiny angel all for me."

"Yes, Victor. All for you. I want you now."

"Lie down on your back, little teacher. I want you too, and I'm going to take you real soon. Just be still and let me savor you a bit longer."

She obeyed.

Victor covered her body with his, kissing her again and again while his strong, calloused hands ran over every inch of her, caressing her breasts, reaching low to cup her buttocks, lifting her so she could feel his thick erection against her belly.

She made a little sound and twined her legs around his.

He lowered her to the bed and pulled back, touching his lips to the skin between her breasts and sliding down the center of her body, past her belly button, to the dark curls between her thighs.

Caroline drew in a deep breath. *I've always wondered what this felt like.*

He licked her lips apart and pressed that bewitching mouth to her clitoris, snaking out his tongue to wet the sensitive nub.

"Ohhhhh," she moaned.

"That's it," he murmured, the vibration of his voice

sending a shock wave through her. "I believe you promised me a scream."

~

That's it, pretty lady. Let me give you pleasure. Feel me touching you, tasting you. Enjoy it.

Victor teased Caroline with his tongue, eliciting a startled squeak of pleasure. She seemed surprised by her reaction to him.

Just as I suspected. Her ex was a selfish asshole, not just a kinky one. No wonder it all fell apart. But she's so responsive. She needs this bad. He breathed over her, stimulating her in yet another way. Each lick elicited a gasp. Each gentle suck a moan of pleasure. She groaned in ecstasy, her hips shifting. Still, despite his best efforts, her peak remained elusive, so he slid two fingers into her.

Caroline's orgasm exploded like a fireball, her sex clamping down hard as a rasping wail of pleasure dropped from her mouth.

Hell yeah. That's what I'm talking about. Before she could come down from it, he replaced his fingers with his erection, easing into her.

She whimpered at the spreading sweetness.

He thrust deep, pulling back to drive in again.

The pressure of his penetration reignited her climax. Every deep thrust wrung new spasms from her until the wet squeezing of her sex proved an unbearable stimulation to him. He rocked in deep one last time and let himself go. *Please, whatever deities there be, let my seed take root in her.*

He kissed her once more as his own climax faded. Then he rolled off, cuddling up against her side and sliding his arm behind her as he touched his lips to her cheek.

"Oh, Victor," she said softly, "that was amazing. I've

never um, done that. It was... it was like nothing I've ever experienced."

Three years and he never went down on her? Not even badly, just... never? "Really?"

"Really."

He blinked. "Why not? You had a long relationship."

She flushed and replied timidly, "I don't know. Remember, his tastes were... well they had more to do with him than me or us. I've wondered, but I was shy to ask."

Victor couldn't keep the smirk from his face. *I knew it.* "Poor William. I would hate it if my former lover looked back and said, in that tepid voice, 'it was okay'. What a sad indictment on the whole relationship."

"Please, let's not talk about William anymore," Caroline whined.

"Sorry," he said automatically, but he didn't feel sorry. He felt pleased with himself. *She'll never have to ask me to taste her. She's delicious... and so responsive. Why wait for her to ask?*

She prodded the conversation back to them. "Seriously, why is it like this between us? So hot and intense?"

Victor pondered the question. "Well, we do have mechanics on our side. For some reason, our bodies fit together exceptionally well." At the thought of how exquisite the fit really was, his exhausted sex tried to rise again. "But there's also the fact that we're finally indulging a years'-long attraction."

"Right." she sighed, melting into his embrace.

"This is going to be a wonderful weekend."

"I know."

He took a deep breath. "I think there's another reason as well."

"What's that?"

"Can't you guess?"

She shook her head.

55

"Little teacher, I'm madly in love with you."

She turned her head and looked him in the eyes, her own filled with such uncertainty and disbelief. "Oh, Victor I wish I could say the same but…"

He silenced her with a kiss. "I know, Caroline. I know it's too soon. You're still hurting, not ready yet. I didn't tell you to pressure you."

"Why did you then?"

He stroked her cheek. "Because when things end, it's sad, even if it really is the right thing. When you're sad, it's good to know someone loves you. You don't have to love me back right now; I didn't expect that you would. I just want you to relax, let me love you, let me spoil you and make you feel good. When the time is right, I'm sure the feelings will come. I'm willing to wait for them. You'll love me, Caroline, when you're ready; I know it. It doesn't have to be today."

She tucked one arm behind her head. "Wow. It's a lot to take in."

"You deserve it, you know. You deserve to be loved," he insisted.

"I don't think I ever have been," she replied.

"Yes, you have," he argued.

She shook her head. "He didn't love me."

He laid his hand on her cheek and turned her to face him so he could look into her eyes again. "No, he didn't, but I did. I always have. That's why I could never stop coming to see you even when I didn't have time to take your classes anymore. I needed to be near you whenever I could. I've amazed myself being this bold. I was sure you would refuse me, but you were so pretty, so sad. I had to take the risk and look at us now. We're here together in this bed, and my baby could be growing inside you already. I have no regrets. Do you?"

"Of course not." The sorrow in her eyes enticed him. "You're too good for me, Victor."

"No way!" he insisted. "You're just what I want, any way I can get you."

She traced his lips with one fingertip and then cupped his cheek. "Kiss me."

He did.

She tried to roll into his arms, but he pinned her hip to the bed, then lifted her and tucked a pillow underneath. "Stay. Don't waste it."

"Right."

He crawled back over her, laying his mouth on hers again and again. He was spent, flaccid after such passionate lovemaking, but his love was overflowing. He poured it all on her, filling her heart as surely as he had her body moments ago.

～

It's too much, Caroline thought, feeling guilty as she took it from him knowing she had nothing to give in return. That didn't stop her, greedy monster that she was, from devouring it all. She took his love, absorbed it, let it flow into the parts of her heart where a shy and introverted child had been mocked by prettier and more popular children, where an awkward, bookish teen never got asked to the prom, never went on dates, and at last to where a lonely woman had given herself to a handsome man who had paid attention to her, even though she had always known his interest was weak, his tastes incompatible. *I thought it was the best I would ever get.*

Being passionately loved by the shy and beautiful creature in her arms far exceeded her expectations. In that moment she did love him, just a little. *It will take time for that seed to grow, but I'll nurture it because he deserves my love too.*

57

Saturday evening, Caroline's cell phone rang. She fished it out of her bag, which she'd dropped on the floor in the middle of the room, and pushed the button.

"Hey, Maggie, what's up?" she asked.

"Just wondering where you were. I haven't heard from you in days. I went to your house but no one was there. Did you go to visit your family?"

"No. I'm out of town. Is anything wrong?" Caroline asked, wondering if some emergency had arisen.

"No, nothing," Maggie reassured her. "I just wanted to be sure you were okay, what with William and all. I've never been so pissed at anyone in my life. Stupid Jessica. I've been talking to Sophie, and we both think she should be out of the group for what she did."

"William who?" Caroline quipped.

Maggie scoffed into the phone.

"No, seriously. I'm not sorry at all. He wasn't good enough for me." She glanced at the kitchen where Victor stood at the sink, washing dishes.

His eyes lingered on her with an intense expression.

Okay, we're a couple. He's my boyfriend. I might already be pregnant. It's time to stop keeping it a secret and Maggie is a good first person to tell. "Actually, I've completely moved on. I have a new man in my life, Maggie."

"Really?" She could visualize her friend's black eyebrows shooting upward. "Already?"

"Yes. His name is Victor. He's pretty amazing. We're spending Thanksgiving together," she replied, winking at him.

"With his family?"

"No. All alone in a little cabin in the woods."

Silence. Now she could almost see Maggie's jaw hanging open at that unexpected news. "Whoa."

"Yeah." Caroline could feel a slow, glowing smile spreading across her face.

"Uh, are you sure that's a good idea?" Maggie asked, more curious than concerned if her tone provided any indication.

"Yes. I needed this in a big way," Caroline replied, trying not to melt at the memory of just how tenderly Victor had loved her.

The caution increased in Maggie's voice. "Maybe, but is it fair to... Victor, did you say his name was?"

"Yes, Victor. He knows all about what happened. He's okay with helping me get over it. He's wonderful," she gushed.

Victor walked towards her, sliding his arms around her while she talked.

She leaned into his warmth with a comfortable groan.

"Is it a secret?" Maggie asked, "I mean, I would love to tell Sophie. She's worried about you too."

Victor's mouth caressed the side of her neck.

"No, it's no secret. I want everyone to know. Tell Sophie. Tell her I've never experienced anything like this, and no matter what, I can't imagine regretting being this happy."

He nibbled her earlobe.

Oh, God, that's distracting.

"Oh, okay. Well, will I see you Monday night?" Maggie asked.

Caroline paused, trying to make her lips form the answer. "I wouldn't miss it..." She pulled back from Victor's passionate caresses so she could answer coherently.

"So, when do we get to meet your new man?"

"Soon. Let me ask him. Honey?"

He released her ear.

"My friend Maggie wants to know when she can meet you."

"Uh, I don't know. I'm not really good at meeting people." He made an uncomfortable face.

She made a face at him, telling him without words that he was going to have to get over it. *After all, you want to get a job someday. Interviewing with prospective employers is a lot scarier than drinking margaritas with my friends.*

"What did he say?" Maggie demanded

"He's a little shy. He's thinking about it."

Victor's hands wandered scandalously over her body.

"I can see you with a shy guy. That's a good fit."

"Mmm, such a good fit," Caroline moaned.

Victor waggled his eyebrows at her.

"Um, T.M.I. I don't need to know that much," Maggie protested.

Caroline felt too entranced even to be embarrassed. "Sorry. I'm having a hard time concentrating."

"I guess. Listen, I'm going to hang up now. You go... have fun."

"Oh yes," she replied as he cupped her breast. "It's always fun."

"And again with the overshare. Bye, Caroline."

"Bye."

She hung up.

"Did you just tell your girlfriend about me?" Victor met her eyes with a speaking look.

"Of course. Was I not supposed to?"

"No, it's fine. I didn't know you were ready to… go public with this. Good. I can tell my parents. They'll be overjoyed."

"Victor, you're my boyfriend, aren't you?" Caroline demanded.

"Yes," Victor replied, his eyes questioning her question.

"Then what's the big secret? Neither of us is married or a criminal, and we're both mature adults. We have every right to be together if we want to. It's not classified information."

"I like that answer." He grinned, which she found irresistible. She caught his plump lower lip in her teeth, worrying it tenderly. He tugged and she released him so he could kiss her properly.

~

Caroline extended the phone from the pocket of his sweatpants with a wide grin and held it out to him.

Victor took the opportunity to kiss her into a puddle of molten anticipation, and then he called his parents. *I can't wait to tell them all about how I finally won the woman I've adored for so long.* The connection clicked. "Hello, Mom?"

"Victor, darling, how are you?" his mother asked in her soft, low-pitched voice.

"I'm great. How are you?"

"Wonderful," she gushed, "I've just learned a new decoupage technique."

"That's great," he replied, amusement and admiration warring in the background. "I can't wait to see it. Listen, I needed to tell you something."

She must have heard the intense note in his voice. "Oh, did you meet someone?"

How interesting that she figured it out immediately. How did she know I wasn't calling to tell her about a job interview? Victor ran his fingers through Caroline's hair, smoothing the short cap he'd just finished ruffling.

She closed her eyes like a cat and rubbed against his hand.

"No, I've actually known her a long time. It's just that now, we're together. I have a girlfriend, Mom."

"That's great! Does this mean you've finally gotten over that professor?" his mother asked.

Victor grinned. *That will never happen. Guess Mom isn't psychic after all.* "No, she's the one. I did what you said. I told her how I felt, and she agreed that we could... become a couple."

Caroline laid her lips on his neck, teasing him the way he'd teased her.

He wrapped his free arm around her and kissed the top of her head.

"Well, that's wonderful, love. I'm so glad for you. Is that where you are now? With her?" his mother = asked, her voice bright.

"Yes," Victor replied. *Right here with her in my arms.*

"Put her on the phone."

"Caroline?"

She pulled back to meet his gaze.

"My mom wants to talk to you."

"Uh, okay." She shot him a puzzled look but accepted the phone.

~

"Hello, this is Sam Johnston, Victor's mother," a smooth, well-modulated voice spoke into the phone.

"Caroline Jones." She controlled her tone, determined not to give away her discomfort at having this conversation with a woman she didn't know.

"Well, I have to say, I'm glad to talk to you. Victor's been after you for a while."

Though she knew this, it surprised Caroline that Victor had told his mother so much. *Maybe it really is love.* "So I hear. Well, he's got me now." She could feel his touch tingling across her skin.

"Good. He's a good boy."

Good boy? Only if you're his mother. He may be shy, but he's all man to me. She rested her head against his shoulder. "He is. I'm a lucky woman."

"Listen, is he still right there?"

"Uh-huh." This time, Caroline fought to stay focused. *I don't want to sound like an airhead with Victor's mom. That would be no kind of good first impression.*

"I'm going to say something really quiet. I don't want him to overhear. Don't give me away, okay?"

"Sure." She switched the phone to the other ear and took hold of Victor's hand, distracting him from eavesdropping by stroking sexy little squiggles on his skin.

"I'm having a surprise party for Victor's birthday. I hope you can come," Sam explained.

"Naturally," Caroline replied. She discovered that Victor's palm had been deeply marred by a thick, twisting scar. She traced it with one fingertip and then kissed it.

"December tenth, it's a Friday, at seven," Sam said.

"Yes," Caroline agreed idly. She ran her tongue over the scar.

He caught her chin and lifted her face, staring into her eyes with chocolate passion.

She gulped and broke eye contact. *Can't look at him right now. It's too distracting. I'll drown in his affection later.*

"You can help be my cover. Just tell him I've invited you over to meet the family, which I have. Don't tell him it's a party."

"You bet," Caroline agreed, though if she'd been asked to repeat the details she'd just heard, she would have been in deep trouble.

Sam's voice returned to its normal volume. "By the way, I'm an artist and art teacher."

"I'm a teacher too," Caroline replied.

"Yes, I know. English, right?"

"Yes." *Duh. Of course she'd know what you teach. If Victor's told her that much about you, it's no surprise.*

Victor kissed her forehead and released her, striding to the bathroom.

Why couldn't you have done that sooner, silly?

"Well, one thing I like to do is make jewelry. I would love to make some for you," Sam offered, jolting Caroline back into awareness.

"How sweet. Thank you."

"What do you look like?" the woman asked. "It will help me choose a color and pattern."

Uh, where to start with that? "I have dark brown hair."

"Long?"

"Short." She brushed the crumpled locks back into position.

"A bob?" Sam pressed.

Wow, she really does want to know all the details. "No, a pixie."

"Interesting," Sam intoned in a slow voice.

I wonder what she means by that.

"And your eyes?"

"Hazel."

Without the warmth of Victor's nearly constant touch, the cold in the cabin began to creep up on Caroline. She pulled a blanket off the bed and wrapped it around herself.

"What about your complexion?"

"Pale," she admitted. "I burn without tanning most every summer."

"Hmmm. What about your height? Are you tall?"

She suppressed a giggle. *Only if you're from Lilliput.* "Not at all. I'm five-two exactly… in shoes."

A moment of silence ensued and then Sam said, "That's actually a good size for Victor."

"Yes." *Perfect height. Lucky for the two of us.*

"Okay, I'll see what I can come up with."

"That's very nice of you," Caroline replied.

"One more question. What do you like to drink?"

"Anything…" she remembered something important. "Except I'm not doing alcohol these days."

Another pause. "Oh, no problem," Sam said at last.

Shrewd, this one. She thinks everything over. Victor is like that.

"I'll see you on the tenth," Caroline replied, proud that she'd remembered the date at least. *I'd better write that down or I'll forget, and wouldn't that look bad?*

"Okay. Hand me back to Victor, okay?" Sam requested.

"Okay, bye."

Victor had returned, so she passed him the phone and hurried into the kitchen

I'm hungry. All this lovemaking is wearing me out… not that I mind, of course. The clock on the wall read 9:25 pm. She couldn't wait to go to sleep cuddled against him, which she did each night, another first for her.

William always came to my house and left as soon as we were done, she reflected as she tore open a granola bar. She tried to stop comparing the two of them but couldn't. *This sweet new affair leaves the old one completely in the dust. I felt like an experienced woman, but Victor blew all my old expectations out of the water.*

She ate her snack and brushed her teeth while Victor finished his conversation with his parents. Then they curled up together on the sofa bed. Victor pulled her close and closed his eyes.

Caroline stayed awake a while longer. *This is amazing, like nothing I could have imagined. Victor is… he's too good to be true. I'm a lucky, lucky woman.*

~

On Sunday, they gathered the sheets, packed up their suitcases and headed back to the city.

It will be difficult to integrate this idyll into real life, Caroline thought as they pulled into her driveway, *but of course, one can't just escape forever.*

The temperature had risen to a balmy forty-four degrees. Not warm, to be sure, but warm enough for their winter outerwear actually to succeed in its intended task. Caroline slithered out of the truck and headed around to the back to collect her suitcase, but Victor beat her to it.

"A gentleman always carries a lady's bag," he told her as he lifted in one hand.

The thickness of his bicep did amazing things to her lady bits. *And so do his abs… and his narrow waist. Face it, girl, everything about Victor turns you on.* But most of all, his wonderful intelligence and gentle spirit. *Who needs an alpha male when a genuine nice guy wants to share your bed?*

Grinning, she unlocked the door and led him through the kitchen and up the stairs to her bedroom. Once again, he scanned the space as though not sure what to make of it. He set the suitcase on the floor, still looking around the room.

"I guess I'd better go," he said, but something about his tone told her leaving was the last thing he wanted to do.

"I guess," she replied while the whiney kid inside her wailed, *Noooo! Don't leave, Victor!*

He took a step towards her bedroom door. Then another. Then he paused and looked over his shoulder at Caroline.

Her lip trembled and she bit down hard on it.

Without warning, he moved, darting directly into her space until their bodies touched. They threw their arms around each other and began kissing desperately. One would have thought they were separating for years with an ocean between them rather than just the length of a town. They could get together any time, really, but it didn't matter.

Caroline pulled Victor into her bed. They even found it difficult to release each other's mouths long enough to pull their sweaters off so they could touch skin-to-skin.

Caroline's jeans proved to be more difficult. Finally, she just lowered them. She rolled onto her belly and rose to her knees.

Victor knelt behind her, running a gentle hand over her bottom.

Caroline felt neither shame nor modesty knowing he was regarding her private places.

She gasped, hearing his belt jingling as he opened it. "Please, Victor. Now. Take me now," she cried, breathless with desperation.

He obeyed her plea, parting her and sliding deep.

She groaned with relief as Victor began to thrust hard into her. It felt so good to have him there. *We're a perfect match physically, each uniquely shaped to provide the other maximum stimulation.*

They were so turned on, so ready, they approached climax quickly in a flurry of wild thrusts. Caroline cried out as pleasure washed over her.

Victor groaned as his orgasm followed hers. As always, he lowered Caroline onto her back, propping her up and lying close beside her. He kissed her cheeks and temple, making her smile.

"That was a little silly," she said, trying to sound casual.

"I know. I just feel like… if I let you go, if I go home, it will never be the same again," he replied. "It's ridiculous."

He's right, and if it's ridiculous, then I am too because I feel the same way. The realization didn't stop tears from springing to Caroline's eyes. "Victor, do you really have to go?"

"What do you mean?" he demanded, his face twisted into a pleading look. "What else will I do?"

"Can't you just stay here with me, forever?" she begged.

His stroking hands went still. "Is that a rhetorical question, love? It almost sounds like… an invitation. Please tell me if you mean it, Caroline."

She thought for a long moment. *Is this just a rhetorical question or am I asking Victor to move in? I don't know. I didn't want to move in with William, but that was because there was no future in it. Victor made it clear he has permanent intentions towards me. But it wouldn't be right unless I feel the same way towards him. Do I? Well, if not, why am I almost crying at the thought of him driving home, even though he can easily come and see me tomorrow?* "It's not rhetorical. I know people might say it's too soon, but I can't help it. I don't want to let you out of my sight."

She expected him to grin, but he didn't. His eyes bored into hers with molten intensity. "I know what you mean." Then his expression changed, grew considering. "But still, I'm a student, Caroline. I have to go to class, study. Those are difficult things to do when I'm distracted by my beautiful woman." His fingers trailed over her breast and down onto her belly.

"It might be at first, but don't you think you could eventually adjust?" she suggested. "Besides, it's almost Christmas, and then we'll have a month off to get things settled."

"True." He thought some more, eyes far away. "This house is a long way from the university."

"It is." A gnawing sensation grew in the pit of her stomach. Her arms tightened around Victor.

"I'm used to studying at my apartment, going back and forth. I suppose I could use the library instead…"

"You don't sound like you want to. That's okay I guess. Maybe it is too soon." She looked away.

"Caroline… Little teacher." He cupped her face in his hand, turning her towards him. "I want to be here. I'm just trying to work out the details."

"Oh." She exhaled in relief. It sounded like a sob. "I thought you were trying to talk me out of it."

"No. Are you kidding?" Victor chuckled. "Sleeping beside you every night instead of going home to my empty apartment? That's a temptation I can't resist."

"So then?" she pressed.

"So then if you want me here, I'll be here," he replied, his voice confident, his eyes gazing steadily into hers.

"I want you here, Victor." She tugged, but he didn't need the urging. His lips caressed hers with all the heat and intensity she'd grown to expect.

"Okay, just one more question," he said.

"What's that?" she responded, only half listening.

"Why are you doing this? You're not pushing yourself are you?"

"What do you mean?" She shook her head to clear it. *Passion is so hard on the concentration.*

"To move this forward faster." He traced his fingers over her face; eyebrows, nose, cheekbones, lips. "I can see you don't like the idea that I feel more for you than you do for me. You don't have to rush. It's really okay. Take the time. Be sure it's real. Aren't you still hurting?"

She considered. *Am I? I feel like I should be. How could I end such a long relationship without pain?* She prodded at the memories of William but discovered no twinge. *Only wasted time. I don't miss him at all.* She explained. "Dumping William did hurt a little but not in the way you think. I did that hurting a long time ago when I realized that the relationship was waning, and I didn't want to let it go. But then it was gone. The feelings were gone. Even the pain was gone. It all became just a lingering habit. The breakup hurt more like peeling off a Band-Aid. It stings a little, but you want it gone. It's not an injury, so no, I don't think I'm too hurt to want to be with you. I'm not brokenhearted."

Victor wore his concentrating face again, and she smiled to see how well he listened when she talked. He nodded slowly. "Well, that's good. I hate to see you sad."

She stroked the little worry lines between his dark eyebrows and asked, "When have you, apart from that first moment when you walked in on my phone call? Seems to me you've mostly seen me happy. I'm quite... enamored of you Victor. Maybe infatuated. It's not all it could be yet, but it's a start."

He smiled. "It's a good start. So you're really asking me to... move in with you?"

"Yes. I guess I am," she replied.

"And you're doing it because it's really what you want?" he pressed.

"Yes. That I'm sure about," she vowed. *This feels so right. It makes no sense, but it's still real.*

Victor curled up against her, resting his head on her bare shoulder and raining kisses on the side of her neck.

She shivered. *Is there such a thing as afterplay? He brings me down so sweetly.* She hummed as his fingers skimmed her body. Neither of them had an ounce of passion left. They'd burned it all in an inferno of ecstasy, but the random touches afterward felt good, and they enjoyed them. *Real life, I hope you never interfere with my Victor and me. This is as good as it gets.*

Real life, of course, did no such thing, and an uncomfortable thought immediately popped into Caroline's head. "Victor, won't you feel funny?"

"How?" he asked as his fingers skated over her breast.

"It's my house. I own it. You're moving into my space. Doesn't the couple usually choose a place together?"

He considered her words. "Maybe, but I doubt you'd agree to move, and I wouldn't ask it of you. This is a nice house. Right at the moment, I have no money to speak of. My tuition is paid by the Army, and I work some in my dad's shop to cover my car payments and insurance, but I won't really earn anything until after next semester."

"How do you pay for your apartment?"

"It's over my parents' garage." His cheeks colored at the admission.

"Odd living arrangements are normal for a student," she reassured him. "Don't forget these years are an investment in future income."

The two little lines reappeared between his eyebrows in what she was recognizing as his concerned look. "You're right. It is kind of awful to think of living with you but providing nothing."

She kissed the worried 11. "It's temporary, Victor. I know you're not looking for a handout. You'll finish school in less than a year and then we'll be equal partners. In the meanwhile, I'd really love to have you close to me all the time."

The worried line disappeared as his frown transformed into a smile. "Yes. That's what I want as well. Okay, let's try it and see if we can handle it."

She pulled him down so his lips hovered inches from hers and breathed, "Good. I don't think I would let you out of this bed any other way."

CHAPTER 4

$\mathcal{T}$wo weeks later, Victor climbed into his truck and turned the key in the ignition, preparing for the endless drive to campus and mentally running down the list of items he would need, to be sure he hadn't forgotten anything. *Books for my two classes, note-taking materials, lunch, water bottle. Getting to campus has turned into a bit of a chore.* He sighed, but remembering the night he had spent making love to Caroline and then holding her as she slept took away a good bit of the sting. *It is nice to be living in her house.*

Our house, he reminded himself as he drove past yards coated with old, gray snow. *She insists I think of her house as our house. I'm trying but I'll like it a lot better when I'm contributing financially.* He had half a year until he finished his degree, but in the meanwhile, he felt rather odd, like a kept man.

Not that she treats me as one, of course. She's too sweet for that. It warmed him how kind she was to everyone. *Of course, part of that warmth could also be due to the delicious passion we explore each evening.*

He merged onto the freeway, which ran slowly even though the rush hour traffic had already dispersed. *I can't get over how great it is to have, not only a sex partner but a life partner. A girlfriend. I love this.*

A couple of days after their romantic getaway, she'd received a phone call from the doctor's office confirming that all her S.T.D. tests had come back negative. William's betrayal wouldn't hurt him. *I wish it hadn't hurt her. I know she was over him, but breaking up isn't the same as getting cheated on.*

Passing under the gnarled branches of naked oaks interspersed with fragrant, ice-crusted evergreens beneath a blue sky with fat, puffy clouds, Victor pulled into the student parking lot and managed to find a space far at the back. He slung his backpack on and stuck his keys in his pocket as he maneuvered between cars towards the walkways of campus.

Wednesday afternoon and class starts in thirty minutes. Plenty of time to run my little errand. A blast of heat assaulted him as he entered the Liberal Arts building. Unlike his home base in the engineering department—distinguished by tidy notices hung on level corkboards —the walls of this building seemed to assault his senses. Papers in bright colors that served no purpose glared from every wall, offering books for sale, tutoring, and proofreading of essays.

Victor tugged off his gloves, tucked them in his pocket, and unzipped his jacket. *You know, just because it's freezing outside doesn't mean they need to blast the furnaces in here.*

Or maybe they did. Young students in ugly glasses and skimpy clothing stood around rehearsing lines outside the theater. Others pored over textbooks and novels, sipping coffee and munching chips.

Was I ever that young? he asked himself, passing a couple locked in a lusty embrace in the stairwell. They in no way acknowledged his presence.

Shaking his head, Victor quickly climbed the stairs, hoping Caroline would be in her office.

Emerging on the third floor, he proceeded to office 3.102 and heard something he had never expected: the startling sound of Caroline's sweet voice, harshly raised in irritation.

"No, Nick, I told you. You have to provide a works cited page. If you turn it in this way, you're going to get a zero. It's plagiarism the way you wrote it, and that's a violation of intellectual property laws as well as university policy. Do you understand that you could be expelled? I warned you about this a week ago when you turned in your rough draft. You have to cite your sources."

"Oh, come on, Dr. Jones." A low-pitched voice wheedled. "That's stupid. What dusty old professor is going to kick up a fuss about a freshman English paper? Ms. Murphy wouldn't worry about it."

"You're dreaming, Nick. There's not a teacher in this university—especially not Sheridan Murphy—who would pass a paper completely lacking in citations. There's no excuse. The paper is due tomorrow with all the citations in place and correctly formatted. You've had plenty of time to ask for help if you needed it, so I won't give you an extension. You have tonight. Go get it done."

"I have practice tonight," the voice whined.

"If you don't pass this class, you won't be on the team. This is more important. Go talk to your coach. Then get your ass to the library pronto. No excuses. Go."

Victor passed a grumpy-looking young blond man stomping down the hallway in the opposite direction.

"What the hell are you looking at, Mexican?" he snarled.

This one's trouble. Victor shrugged.

"Keep walking then."

Victor kept walking. He had never actually stopped, and this man's permission or lack thereof didn't interest him much. *Not when my lovely lady is just beyond the door.* He knocked once and stepped in.

"Nick, come on... Oh, Victor!" The sight of him turned her worried frown into a charming smile.

"Hi."

"What's up, honey?" she asked.

"I just spoke with my mom. She wants us to come to dinner on Friday. She says you already knew about it."

"Not sure whether I recall but let me put it on my calendar." Smile notwithstanding, her hand trembled as she lifted the pen.

He crossed to the desk and closed his hand around hers. Her fingers felt icy. "Are you all right?"

"Yes, why?" she asked, her eyes skating away.

I know that unhappy expression, little teacher. "I overheard, and you seem stressed." He stroked his thumb over her knuckles.

She closed her eyes. "I love my job. I really do. Sometimes I have to remind myself of that."

He lifted his free hand to her face. She leaned her cheek into his palm. "You're a good teacher. No one can save everyone, especially those who don't want to be saved."

Her lips touched his skin. "You're right. Each person's success is dependent on his or her own choices. You know, I had a student the same time as you who hardly had food to eat. She was so skinny, and she had a little boy to take care of, but she still managed to get straight As.

An image rose in his mind of a strawberry blond with sad turquoise eyes. They had studied together several times. "I remember her. Alyssa, right? What ever happened to her?"

"I don't know." Caroline lifted and dropped her shoulders in a helpless shrug. "I hope she's all right. I've worried about her. I hope she's not going hungry anymore."

Victor recalled more about the fragile woman. Other boys in the class had drooled over her, but not Victor.

Apart from the fact that he could think of nothing but Caroline, something about Alyssa's demeanor told him she wasn't interested in male attention. Maybe his lack of flirtatiousness made her more comfortable with him, because, in the end, they'd become rather friendly. "Let's hope not. She's a really nice person."

"Yes," Caroline agreed, and then added, a bit of sparkle returning to her eyes. "Well, you are too, and you're making the most of your opportunities as well."

"Right." Returning to the present, he grinned. "Well, I have class all afternoon, but I'll see you tonight, okay?"

"Sounds good. I can't wait until you get home. I have plans for you." She gave him a hot look.

"Is that right, little teacher? Mmm, I can't wait."

He leaned across her desk and pressed a quick kiss to her lips before leaving for the engineering building for his afternoon of classes. As he left, he noticed that same blond athlete hanging around near the end of the hallway, a considering expression on his face.

~

Caroline felt a little flushed. *Is it the heat in the building or Victor's kiss?* Her grin widened. *He'll be home tonight for more interesting explorations. I can hardly wait.*

She turned to her planner, intending to record the 'meeting' with Victor's parents...*Victor said I knew. Did I? Sam said something about that, didn't she?* The memory of Victor's caresses heated her even further, but also brought to mind... *It's his surprise party. Yikes, and I almost forgot it.* Her pen hovered over the paper when she noticed a date, two days past, circled in red. *What is that?*

Ah yes, that's the day I was supposed to start my period. A strange sensation of heat whooshed through her head as she realized it hadn't happened yet. *Two days is nothing to get excited about*, she tried to remind herself, but her heart pounded anyway.

Thankful her classes were done for the day, she taped a sign on her door to the effect that office hours were canceled, let the secretary know she was leaving and drove down the street to the store. Her hands shook as she looked at the large array of pregnancy tests available in every price range. In the end, she just closed her eyes and grabbed one, then paid for it and drove home.

But how am I going to do this? she wondered, sitting limp on the sofa in the den, the pink cardboard box clutched in her sweating, trembling hands. *Can I really wait until evening for him to come home?*

She shook her head. *No, I can't wait, and I do it alone either. I need… someone. Sophie? Sophie is in the daycare until six. She can't leave all those kids. Jessica's out, of course. I never want to see her again. Maybe Maggie's available. As a physical trainer, she has flexible hours. If she doesn't have a class right now, maybe she can come over. Yes. That would be good.*

Caroline dialed the number.

"Hello?"

She answered. Thank goodness. "Hi Maggie, it's Caroline." She rose to her feet and crossed the room before turning and heading back the other direction.

"Hi, what's up?" Maggie sounded concerned.

Guess my nervousness was audible. "Um, are you working right now?"

"No, I'm done. Why?"

"I have something really hard that I need to do, and I was hoping for some moral support." Caroline realized her whole body was shaking and sank down on the sofa.

"Oh, sure," Maggie agreed easily. "Where are you at?"

"My home."

"I'll be right there."

Tension settled horribly in the pit of Caroline's stomach while she waited for her friend to arrive.

What if it's nothing? Oh God, what if it's something? She flung herself off the couch and paced nervously again until she heard a knock.

Caroline hurried down the hall to the mudroom and opened the door to receive Maggie's warm hug, grateful for the friends she could count on to support her. "I'm so glad you're here."

"You look like shit," the tall young woman replied with her usual candor. "Are you sick?"

"No. I'm not. I…" She closed her eyes, not knowing how to continue.

"What?" Maggie pressed, urging Caroline into the kitchen.

"I need to take a pregnancy test." Caroline spat the words out fast before they could get stuck again. "I'm scared to death."

"Oh God. Are you sure?" The concern in Maggie's eyes made Caroline feel more supported.

"No. Hence the test," she pointed out.

"Oh, right," Maggie sighed. "Jeez, everyone's pregnant."

"Who?" Nerves overtook her again and she began a babble. "I don't know of anyone other than me… if I am, but I might not be. I know you're not since your boyfriend is still abroad. Sophie's man is deployed, and I don't think Jessica would tolerate a pregnancy for long and…"

"Selene," Maggie admitted, frowning with disapproval as she cut off Caroline's mad rush. She shook her head as though to clear out unwanted images. Her dark hair swirled around her shoulders before settling back into place perfectly. "She and Dad are expecting. That's why they got married so fast. Can you believe at my age that I'm about to be a big sister? Oops." Maggie rolled her eyes.

Ah, that makes sense. Well, except why it bothers Maggie so much. Her dad is young and… pretty hot. So for him to start again isn't so strange. I'm sure she'll adjust. Meanwhile, she thinks this is an accident I'm upset about, so I should explain what I'm up to. "I'm sorry your dad's situation upsets you, Maggie," Caroline squeezed her friend's arm, "but this is different."

"In what way?" Maggie's far-away expression returned to reality.

"I did it on purpose," Caroline admitted, not sure why it made her cheeks burn so fiercely.

Maggie stared, open-mouthed, and finally blurted, "Whoa. Why?"

This explanation is getting tedious. "I'm running out of time. I'm thirty-three. I don't want to miss out. So I'm really nervous now."

To her credit, Maggie only stared at her in jaw-flapping shock for a couple more seconds. Then she firmed her resolve, heaved a deep breath and replied, "Yeah, I bet. Okay, I'm here now, so you'd better get it done before you make yourself sick with worry. Do you know what to do?"

"Yes." Caroline picked up the box from the coffee table, noting with nervous amusement how it had been mangled in her tight grip as she read the instructions over and over.

"Okay, get to it. I'll be right in the den waiting for you when you're done."

Waiting and probably trying to process whether this is a silly idea she should be concerned about. "Thanks, Maggie."

Caroline hurried into the first-floor powder room. The test only took a few seconds to perform, but it would be three minutes before the results appeared. Unable to stand watching it, she abandoned the stick on the counter and left the room. Her nervous trembling had transformed into a shaking so hard, she struggled to remain upright as she staggered down the hall to the den.

Maggie wrapped her arms around her and led her to the leather sofa. "Sit down before you fall," she said gently, urging Caroline off her wobbly knees and plunking down beside her. "So Victor's more than just your lover, isn't he? He's supposed to be your baby daddy."

"Yes," Caroline admitted, "that's the plan."

Maggie's expression vacillated from alarm to concern to consideration.

I wonder what all that means. I suppose, after I wasted so much time with William, she doubts my judgment in the relationship department. I can't say I blame her.

To her credit, all Maggie said was, "How's it going?"

Glad to have something other than her nerves to focus on, Caroline began to babble. "Great. I want to be with him all the time. He's the sweetest guy. I'm so happy."

Maggie smiled gently. "That's what you deserve. I'm glad for you."

"You know what? He loves me. He tells me every day." *I hope that's not a secret. I don't think it is… geez, even my thoughts are babbling.*

The tepid smile grew wider. "Good. You need that too. It's good to love someone before you make a baby together, I think."

It is. Knowing how deeply Victor cares for me makes the whole thing seem possible. The baby, the family, the life I never thought I'd have. So why am I holding back? "I haven't told him I love him," Caroline blurted.

Maggie tilted her head. "Why not? You do, don't you?"

Slow down, mental tornado. I need words that make sense. Though the thought storm raged unabated, Caroline picked a bit of meaning out of the swirl. "I don't know. It's been so soon after that other... mess. I don't want this to be a rebound thing."

Maggie rejected that comment with a sharp shake of her head. "That's not your way, Caroline. I can't imagine you being intimate with someone for that reason. There must be something deeper. Have you only known him a few weeks?"

Caroline frowned. Remember, they don't know the story. They don't know who Victor is to you. "No, I've known him for years. He was my student."

"Oh?" The girl's black eyebrows rose.

"He's not a kid though. He's over thirty himself."

A chuckle containing much relief escaped Maggie, and she leaned back against the leather upholstery. "Ah, okay. You know, you could probably go look at that thing now."

"Oh God. Oh, I can't do it. What if it's negative?" The very thought made her trembling increase. To steady herself, she clenched her hands around a pillow printed with a snowy scene.

"It's really not a big deal if it is." Maggie pointed out. "It just means you and Victor get to have fun trying for another month. You have a lot of months before you turn thirty-five. Even after, most likely it will still be fine."

"That's true." She tried to get up, but her wobbly legs wouldn't hold her.

Noticing, Maggie offered, "Do you want me to go?"

"Please?" Caroline begged.

Athletic as always, her friend bounced to her feet and walked through the door. Less than a minute later she returned, sitting down beside Caroline and putting her arms around her. "Congratulations. You're a mommy."

Caroline sucked in a noisy breath and froze, her fingers icy and a strange whooshing noise sounding in her ears. Her mind blanked for a moment and then roared back to life in a gush of babbling thoughts that left her shaken.

Maggie released her, peering into her face with concern, and then patted her knee. "What's wrong? Are you overwhelmed?"

More than I realized. How can I want something so bad, and then it happens, and then everything changes? I still want this baby, so much, but… Suddenly, Caroline felt vulnerable.

Single and pregnant. For some, it's a tragedy, a nightmare. I chose it as a possibility, but it's not what I want. What will the outcome be? Can I do this alone? Tears burned but she blinked them back.

Though rationally she knew that, as a professor, she had the best possible situation in which to raise a child alone—a decent income and plenty of days off—it didn't seem like enough. *I don't want to do this alone, but Victor and I are so new, so unsettled. It might end. Oh God.*

Caroline closed her eyes as her willpower splintered. *I'm not going to cry… I'm not…* A noisy sob broke free.

"Caroline," Maggie's strong hand gripped her shoulder hard, cutting through her maelstrom. "Caroline, what's wrong? This is what you wanted, right?"

"It's… it's Victor," she whispered, her voice shattering over every syllable.

"What about him?" Maggie gave Caroline another puzzled look.

Caroline fisted the fabric of the sofa pillow and gulped air, trying to steady herself enough to express her vague, swirling fear as coherent speech. "What if he changes his mind about this, about us? I'm really going to need him now."

Maggie regarded Caroline with a considering expression. "He loves you, right?" the younger woman asked.

"He says so," Caroline replied.

But how can I know? her insecurity wailed. *How can I*

be sure? People claim to love each other all the time for reasons that have nothing to do with honesty. Though she realized her concern had nothing to do with what she knew of Victor, it didn't matter. Fear had taken hold of Caroline and refused to let her go.

"You're a lovable person," Maggie pointed out. "Not to mention that he agreed to this… idea. I doubt he's going anywhere."

At last, the source of the wild feelings gelled. "But he doesn't know how I feel," Caroline sniffled, steeled herself, and added, "What if he gets sick of waiting for me to make up my mind?"

Maggie's lips crimped. "Then you would lose him, wouldn't you?"

Caroline's hard-won calm collapsed into a flood of new tears.

Maggie wrapped her arms around her friend, motherly despite being over a decade younger. "See, I think you know how you feel. You wouldn't be crying so hard at the mere thought of losing him if you didn't love him."

"But how can I be sure?" Caroline rose from the sofa in nervous agitation and began to pace again, wobbling with every step.

"Well," Maggie said, considering, "a lot of people think that love is how happy someone makes you feel. I don't think I believe that though." She grabbed Caroline's wrist and pulled her friend back onto the couch.

Caroline lowered her eyebrows. "Why not?"

"Because of my parents," Maggie explained. "See, they weren't 'in love' when they got married. Mom was pregnant, and Dad's a responsible guy. The thing is, he had a choice. He could have become bitter about being married to a woman he didn't love, but that's not what happened. He decided to love her, and after a while he did. It was a choice."

"Chose to love someone?" Caroline's overwhelmed mind refused to grasp the radical concept.

"It doesn't make sense, does it, based on what fairy tales tell us? But it was real," Maggie explained. "When she passed away, he grieved until I was afraid he would die of it. I think if it hadn't been for me, he would have. I'm thankful he's got Selene now, even if I seem uncomfortable. She makes him happy. But here's the thing: real love isn't about what the other person does for you. Not only. It's give and take, and above all, it's a choice."

At last, Maggie's words began to penetrate the frantic swirling of Caroline's thoughts. She wiped at her cheeks. "Yes, I think you're right. Victor told me not to push myself, just to let him love me without trying to reciprocate because it's what I needed."

Maggie grinned. "That's how you know he really loves you. If you care more for someone else's happiness than your own, that's love. It's even better when they love you back. When there's passion between you, that's best of all, but at the heart of it, love is giving as much as you take."

"Is that how it is with you and Jan?" Caroline blurted.

"Yes," Maggie said, her eyes going distant as she thought about her dearly loved boyfriend, currently stuck in faraway Sweden.

"Okay." Caroline's tears began to slow, though her breathing remained ragged. "So, what does that mean for me?" *I'm taking relationship advice from a 21-year-old. Goodness, I'm behind.*

Maggie visibly shook off her reminisces and returned her attention to the conversation. "It means you can choose. Do you want to love Victor?"

"Yes," Caroline replied firmly. *To make a family, to love and be loved by someone, not to settle, but to forge strong, unbreakable bonds. There are no words for how much I want that.*

84

I stopped dreaming of it, knowing a relationship with William would always be more complicated and unsettled, but even in this short span of days, Victor has proven he fits neatly into my heart and life. But what if he changes his mind? What if...

"Do you respect him?" Maggie continued, cutting into Caroline's thoughts before they could gallop off on another wild tangent. "Is he a good man?"

"Oh yes." Caroline nodded eagerly. *That much I know for sure. Honest, hardworking, ambitious and kind. What more could anyone want? His handsome face and toned muscles are just the icing on the cake.*

"Do you want him to be happy?" Maggie studied Caroline's face, as though to gauge her reaction to the question.

"Yes." *So much. He smiles with that shy, sincere grin, and I can't help but melt. I love to see it. I love to see him happy. I love to kiss him... I, I, I. Caroline, do you ever think of anyone but yourself? You're so self-centered.* She drew in a shuddering breath and released it in a whoosh. "That's selfish though," she admitted at last. "I want him to be happy so he'll stay with me."

Maggie gave her a speaking glance Caroline couldn't interpret. With a sigh, the girl continued. "That's okay. You actually want him happy?"

"Well, yes."

"What would make him happy?"

It only took a moment to realize the answer. "For me to be proud of him. I think that's what he's wanted all along." *All the lingering glances, all the questions about how an excellent essay could be even better. The time he spent hovering around my office, even when his 'question' was dubious at best. He just wanted to be near me. There's so much evidence.* Her lips twisted in a wry parody of a grin. "Well, that and to sleep with me."

Maggie snorted. "Well he's done that, and from our previous indiscreet conversation, I'd say the sex is a win

SIMONE BEAUDELAIRE

for you both. What about the other. Are you proud of him, proud to be his woman?"

Caroline thought of all he had accomplished. *Military service, entering school at a more mature age instead of assuming it was too late, throwing himself into learning—far beyond the minimum—so that now, he's nearly finished with his degree. Not to mention he's just generally being a fantastic human being.* She grabbed another tissue from the box and blew her nose in a noisy honk.

Maggie feigned a gag.

Snickering at her friend's silliness, Caroline nonetheless answered in all honesty, "Why not? Anyone would be ecstatic to have a man like Victor."

Maggie nodded knowingly. "See, you love him already, you just don't want to admit it. Why is that?"

Why, Caroline? Why would you hold this back? You want the family this represents, and you've always wanted a man like Victor—tender, loving, smart, funny and kind—so why are you afraid to do your part?

The answer dawned on her. "I've never given my heart before. It's scary not to know what the response will be."

"You do know what the response will be," her common sense reminded her. "You know Victor will treasure every bit of you, even the bits you don't appreciate. All you have to do is return the favor, and it's exactly what you want. Don't miss out by being a chicken."

Though she knew her rational mind made an excellent point, the wailing wimp inside her threatened to turn her stomach inside out at the very idea of so much trust. "It's hard," she added.

"Never gave your heart?" Maggie frowned. "What about…"

"No," she interrupted. "I never loved him. I never said I did. He never said so either. I don't know what that was, but it wasn't love."

86

"Okay." Maggie let her line of questioning rest.

Thank goodness. William has no place in this discussion.

And yet, having raised his specter, her former boyfriend refused to be banished. *I wonder if my concerns about Victor come from my time with William.* Seeing a correlation, Caroline finally dared ask herself the question she'd been pondering for weeks. "Why did I waste years on someone I don't love? Why did I get intimate with him?"

Maggie twisted her lips to one side in an expression of disgust and loathing. "Who knows? There are probably lots of reasons, and some of them don't make sense later. They just become regrets. You're not the only person who's ever made that mistake." The girl's voice turned dark.

What? But I thought... "I thought you were only with Jan."

The girl looked away, cheeks coloring. "Yes, he was my first, but not my only partner." Maggie closed her eyes. "After he went back to Sweden, I thought we were done. It's just too far away, so I tried to move on, and in the end, I slept with this other guy. It was really stupid, and I hated it. Thankfully, Jan was willing to forgive me." She scrubbed her hand over her face. "Better Jan from across an ocean than anyone else."

"I can understand that," Caroline said. *And why did I not know this? Was I so wrapped up in my own drama that I ignored my friends? Shame on me.* "Is he coming back?"

"Not to stay. Not yet. We've applied for a fiancé visa. He comes to visit often. He came for Dad's wedding back in October." Maggie rubbed the end of her nose.

A soft clunk sounded at the far end of the house and then muffled footsteps crossed the kitchen floor tiles. Both women turned and saw the door into the den opening.

"Victor?" Caroline asked, startled.

Sure enough, the topic of their conversation strode into the room. "Hi, Caroline," he said, calm as anything.

He has no idea that... everything is about to change. Still a bit fuzzy after the emotional storm she'd endured, Caroline blurted, "Why are you home so early?"

The graceless question drew his attention straight to her face and he frowned, but answered sensibly, "Class was canceled. I wanted to see you, but you were gone, so I decided to come home too." His eyebrows drew together. "Why are you crying?"

She drew in a lungful of air, trying to ignore the way it shuddered past her spasming throat. "It's nothing. I'm fine."

Her friend made an incredulous sound.

Victor glanced, froze and turned slowly to face the source of the sound. "Maggie? What are *you* doing here?"

The girl's gaze shifted from her friend to him and back. "Caroline, you didn't tell me your boyfriend was *this* Victor."

"You know each other?" Caroline asked, puzzled.

"Yes. I have quite a few clients. He's one of them," Maggie explained, and the concerned face she'd been wearing since her arrival dissolved into a broad grin.

Caroline blinked. "Oh, I didn't know."

Maggie's smile twisted sidewise in her attempt to hold in a giggle. "Since I know now this is the man we're talking about, I think you can count on him. He's a really good guy."

Caroline barely heard Maggie's comment as she walked, dreamlike, into Victor's arms.

He enfolded her gently. "What's up?" he asked.

The melting chocolate warmth in his eyes soothed Caroline's nerves until she felt like a puddle of molten happiness. She cupped his cheek in one hand, grateful for his smaller stature so she could touch him easily. "I have to tell you something. Two things really."

"Okay, shoot." He smoothed a lock of dark hair off her forehead.

"First of all," She stopped and looked up into his beautiful dark eyes. With one fingertip she traced the full curve of his lower lip. "Victor, do you still love me?"

"Yes, of course. Why?"

My poor baby. I have him so worried and confused. "Because I love you too," she replied.

He blinked. At first, it seemed, the words didn't register fully. Then he sucked in a noisy breath. "Do you really? Are you sure?"

"Yes."

A tentative, startled expression spread across his face. "Say it again. I want to hear it."

"I love you." She beamed through her tears. *He makes me happier than anything I've known, and now I've done the same for him. I mean that much to him.*

"Oh, sweet woman." His lips curved upward until he was glowing with joy. Then he lowered his mouth to hers, sealing their love with a kiss of softly startling tenderness.

After several long moments, Caroline released Victor's mouth and continued. "And that brings me to my second piece of news. It's really little though... Actually, it's little now, but it's going to get bigger and bigger."

He drew in his breath. "Are you saying...?"

"Yes." She guided his hand to her belly. "I'm pregnant."

"And that's why you were crying?" he asked as he stroked the tiny convexity that did not yet signal her condition.

"Kind of." She bit her lip and broke eye contact, studying the buttons on his shirt. "I was worried that you might not still want me now that our goal has been accomplished."

"Caroline, that's ridiculous," he scolded tenderly. "I want you no matter what. I've always wanted you. I offered to give you a baby because it's what you wanted; it was your goal. Being with you has always been mine. I'm going to assume that this is just your hormones going crazy, because you know I love you and want to be with you forever."

"Okay." She snuggled close to him.

He hugged her tight.

~

Maggie considered how to make a quick and graceful exit. *Now that Caroline has told Victor her news, I'm sure they're going to want me to leave so they can savor it in private. Shall I slip away? They probably won't even notice.*

She shook her head. *I'll wait and say goodbye. After that huge emotional storm, she's going to need a lot of reassurance. Of course Victor will give it to her, but I know she'll want her friends' endorsement too.* She glanced at the couple.

Victor held Caroline close, his hand circling on her back. Her head rested on his chest.

It struck Maggie how good they looked together. *I never really cared for Caroline's old boyfriend. For one thing, William's towering height doesn't suit her one bit. Victor's solid 5'7, on the other hand, seems perfect.* Caroline looked small and protected in his arms, but not ridiculous.

He stared down at her with a fierce, passionate expression, but his hand stroked her back gently. *He looks like a kind man who is desperately in love. Perfect. William always was a little chilly and condescending with Caroline, as though he didn't think much of her, and that bothered me. This is much better. Caroline deserves to be deeply loved, and Victor, not William, is the man who will give her that.* "Okay, guys," she said. "Congratulations. I'm going now."

Caroline laid her lips briefly on Victor's chest before

stepping out of his embrace and turning to hug her friend.

Maggie squeezed her warmly. "I'm glad you're with Victor. This is just what you need."

"I know. I'm really happy." She smiled through a veil of tears.

Wow, that's powerful. Thank goodness they found each other. This is going to be great for them both.

As though he couldn't stand not touching her another moment, Victor slipped his arms around Caroline from behind, pulling her back into his embrace.

"I'm glad for you too, Victor," Maggie added, giving her shy client an encouraging smile. "This is the professor you told me about, right?"

"Yes." His fingers laced through Caroline's and he rested his chin on her shoulder. The couple wore matching expressions of deep happiness.

"I wish I'd known," Maggie said. "I would have tried to set you up ages ago." She pondered another moment. "Caroline, why don't you bring him to our Monday night get-together? Sophie would like to meet him."

"Okay, I can do come." Victor agreed, uncomfortable but willing. "Except—that Jessica—I don't want to meet her."

Maggie compressed her lips. *Nasty bitch. We should have dumped her trashy ass ages ago.* "No. Everyone is in agreement. That kind of behavior won't be tolerated. It was necessary for Caroline to break up with that creep, but sleeping with other people's boyfriends makes a person untrustworthy, and we need to surround ourselves only with people we can trust."

"Right," Caroline agreed. "No more bad friends or boyfriends." She squeezed Victor's hand.

"Exactly," he agreed.

And I can see that you, mister, want to be a very good boyfriend. Excellent. "See you two later."

"Bye, Maggie." Caroline smiled and waved.

"See you soon," Victor added.

Maggie made her way back into the kitchen and out the door, smiling to herself. *How great is this?*

Once the door closed and the battered pickup rumbled away, Caroline turned in Victor's arms to receive the fierce, burning kiss he lavished on her mouth.

"Well, little teacher, I'm finding the thought that I've sowed my seed in you very arousing. Would you be willing to let me take you to bed and show you how much?"

"Oh yes," she sighed. "Let's go right away."

Victor surprised her by scooping her into his arms and carrying her.

At first, she felt a thrill of fear, but his biceps flexed beneath her, easily bearing her weight, and she knew he wouldn't drop her. She leaned her cheek tenderly against his shoulder. *Like a romantic movie... and I'm the heroine.*

Beside their bed he set her on her feet and skimmed his hands under her clothing to undress her, lightly trailing his fingers over her fit, curvy body.

"I understand now why you look so good," he commented. "You work hard at it don't you?"

He noticed. She beamed. "Yes, with Maggie's help. I told her I wanted to stay in shape as I got older, but I didn't want a hard body. Just a toned one."

"Looks like she got it just right. You're slim but curvy in all the right places." His eyes touched those places with palpable heat.

The knowledge that he would soon put his hands on them made her feel even warmer. "It's all going to change, Victor," she reminded him, her smile spreading until her cheeks ached.

"I know." His tawny hand pressed against her pale belly. It lay nearly flat from hipbone to hipbone.

In the next few months, it will swell with our baby. She felt a thrill of excitement that perfectly matched the expression on Victor's face.

"How lovely you'll be. I can't wait to see it."

"Me either," she agreed. *To watch myself swell with the child I've wondered if I would ever have. She's in there... or he... growing, developing, preparing to become part of my family—our family. The family we're making together.*

Victor's tender eyes darkened with desire. "Get on the bed, little teacher. I want you." He pulled back the blankets, idly grinning at the pattern of blue and green triangles on the new bedspread they'd bought.

Our bed now, not just mine. I love that. She plunked down on the mattress, kneeling while Victor stripped off his clothing. Then she reached out her arms to him.

He approached, touching his mouth to hers for a long, tender kiss.

Victor has been so sweet, taking his time, loving me, pleasuring me, giving and giving. I want to give him something back. Releasing his mouth, she held him still in front of their bed while her mouth traced over his face, teasingly licking his chin. She bit his neck like a pocket-sized vampire until she left a tiny mark there.

Victor groaned.

With her lips and tongue, Caroline traced the hard muscles of his chest and belly before dipping even lower. Feeling confident in her abilities and aggressively amorous, she opened her mouth over his sex, engulfing him in wet heat and sucking him deep. She pulled back slowly, keeping suction on him, trailing her lips over his hardened flesh, until only his head remained in her mouth. Then she plunged deep again. Her tongue caressed and circled him. With her free hand, she stroked and cradled his testicles, rewarding them for giving her what she had so desperately wanted.

~

An agony of pleasure dragged Victor into its vortex. *Not every woman knows how to go down on a man with such passion and skill. She must be doing this to show how much she loves me.* The realization made the act—already hot enough to strain his endurance—even hotter. "Caroline," he groaned, "I can't hold on much longer. Do you want me to let go?"

She considered, her tongue swirling on the sensitive tip of his sex. "If you want. We can do this either way."

"Let me go, little teacher. I have to be inside you." He eased back and climbed onto the bed beside her.

She urged him down on his back and straddled his slim hips.

Victor cupped Caroline, pressing his fingers to her intimate flesh to be sure she was wet enough. Her moisture coated his fingertips, and her muscles clenched. He gave her what she wanted, guiding his straining erection to the opening of her body and rocking gently upward into her ready little passage.

"Oh!" she gasped as Victor penetrated her deep in a single sure stroke. "That feels so good."

One nice thing about this position, Victor reflected as Caroline began to move on him, *is that it allows space for me to help her to come.* He did just that, finding her clitoris and stroking it in the way he had learned she liked. He could feel her intimate flesh moving as his thick sex thrust in and pulled back.

"I love you, Victor," she moaned as her orgasm drew closer.

"I love you too, Caroline," he replied as he brought her to the glorious explosion he had been stoking. The tightening of her sex on him proved to be too much; too much pleasure, too much emotion. Victor came with her, holding her hips tight as he thrust to the hilt in her and released.

A great deal of time passed before either of the lovers returned to awareness. Caroline lay on Victor's chest, her head over his heart. Both his hands rested on her back.

She kissed his chest. He wrapped his arms around her and hugged her.

CHAPTER 5

On Friday evening, Caroline and Victor drove to his parents' house. Caroline's stomach swooped and her fingers trembled with nerves, of course, but she wanted to meet his family, nonetheless.

As they drove into a neighborhood of small, one-story houses with immaculate, snow-covered yards, Caroline asked, "Victor, are we going to tell them about the baby?"

"I don't know," he replied. "We can if you want to."

She bit her lip, considering her options. "I don't know if I'm ready for that." *Please don't be disappointed.*

"Well, let's just go with the flow then." He reached across to squeeze one hand. "If the time seems right, and you want to say something, say something. If not, well, it's really early yet. There's no rush. A lot of people wait a couple of months before they tell anyone."

"Okay." *Thank goodness. I need to start having faith in Victor. He doesn't sweat the small stuff.*

They pulled up in front of a little yellow box of a house that glowed like sunshine—even at dusk—against the whiteness of snow piled up in the yard.

Victor opened the door for Caroline, sliding his arm around her waist as she emerged. He kissed the top of her head. "They're going to adore you, you know," he informed her.

She cuddled close to his side. "I hope so," she replied, far from certain.

"Hey," Victor stopped moving and tipped Caroline's chin upward to meet his eyes.

Tenderness threatened to melt her into a little Caroline puddle, right there in the snow.

"All they've ever wanted is for me to be happy, to be loved. You make me happy, and you love me. That's enough."

"Even though I'm older than you, your former professor and pregnant when we've only been together a few weeks?" she blurted, nerves finally overpowering the calm, reasonable things she kept telling herself.

Victor chuckled at her blunt assessment of their relationship. "I told you my mom's a hippie. She loves it when I do unexpected, unconventional things."

Caroline didn't answer.

Victor unlocked the door, still holding her close, and escorted her inside.

Thick blackness rendered the room invisible. Victor froze, his fingers tightening on hers.

He has no idea what's about to happen. Caroline couldn't quite suppress a grin, despite her nerves.

Suddenly the lights flared on—temporarily blinding after the darkness—and dozens of voices yelled, "Surprise! Happy birthday! ¡Feliz Cumpleaños!"

Victor's jaw dropped. He glanced at Caroline, his expression a fake glower. Then he squeezed her fingers a little tighter as members of his huge extended family came forward to hug him and shake her hand and be introduced. At least thirty men, women and children—some with dark hair and tawny skin, others redheaded and pale—shouted to each other in English and Spanish, all gabbling at once as they crushed Victor in hug

97

after hug. His aunties kissed his cheeks until his skin glowed pink and red with lipstick marks.

The last to approach—a couple in their early fifties—had to be his parents. Victor's father, small like his son, but much darker, his jet-black hair streaked with gray, shook Caroline's hand and quietly introduced himself. "Rafael Martinez. Pleased to meet you, Caroline." He pronounced his name with a strong Spanish inflection, but his accent softened for everything else.

"Pleased to meet you," she replied, responding to his shyness with her own.

He smiled.

Next came a tall woman, much taller than her partner, with a mass of wavy red hair, fading to silver at the temples. She wore a long-sleeved white peasant blouse with a long purple skirt and a black and silver belt that could only be handmade.

"Sam Johnston." She gave Caroline a hug, leaving behind a waft of incense. "I'm so glad finally to meet you."

"Pleased to meet you too," Caroline replied, startled but not unduly upset. *Looks like I'm being given the benefit of the doubt. How different from my own mother.*

"Thanks for not giving away the surprise. The look on Victor's face was priceless." The woman grinned.

"It was." Caroline slipped her arm around Victor's waist.

He chuckled. "Yeah, Mom. You got me good. Listen, I want to introduce Caroline to *Abuelita*."

"Sure. She's in her usual spot."

Interesting, Caroline thought. *Victor pronounced the Spanish word like a native speaker despite his everyday speaking voice being completely Midwestern, without a hint of any other accent. He's truly bilingual. What a study that would make... Bilingualism in the upper Midwest. I wonder how many languages would be represented.*

Caroline put a lid on her nerdy tendencies as Victor

walked her through a small living room painted in a
warm terracotta shade, over an oak floor adorned with
a hand-woven rug. Three ceramic sunbursts with faces
on them hung above a mission style sofa and two chairs
with wooden arms.

In a small leather recliner in the corner near the
window sat an elderly Mexican woman, her white hair
pulled back into a bun. Her vacant blue eyes revealed
her blindness.

"¿Abuelita?" Victor began in Spanish.

"¡Victor! ¿Como estas, mijito?"

"Muy bien. ¿Y usted?" He kissed her cheek.

"Bien, bien."

"Abuela, le voy a presentar a Carolina. Es mi amor."

Caroline tried hard to remember what she had
learned. *It's been a long time since Intermediate Spanish II.
This is Caroline. She is my beloved*, she mentally translated, glowing at the tender introduction.

The woman extended a gnarled hand.

Caroline took it gently in both of hers.

"Mucho Gusto, Carolina. Soy Juana Martinez."

"Mucho gusto, señora," Caroline replied, pro-
nouncing the words with care.

"¿Amas a Victor?" the older woman asked bluntly.

Do you love Victor? Caroline mentally translated. *How
do I answer?* "Si. Lo amo mucho," Caroline admitted
after an awkwardly long pause. *I think that's how I say I
love him a lot.*

"Muy bien." She patted Caroline's hand.

Having exhausted all the Spanish she could remember, Caroline fell silent.

Victor hugged her closer, continuing a conversation
she could almost understand. *I need to refresh my lan-
guage skills.*

They mingled for a while, Victor introducing her to
relatives ranging in age from college to middle age, all
in English, though many of them spoke with an accent.

Caroline smiled, but after the first six or seven, the names and faces blended together, and her overwhelmed thoughts began to whirl around like a tornado that made her dizzy. The dizziness quickly transferred itself to her stomach, where it churned up an edge of lingering nausea. *Oh dear. Morning sickness in the evening? Now what?*

A mouthwatering scent of savory spices filtered into the living room. Caroline's stomach growled, momentarily quelling her discomfort.

"Dinner, everyone," Sam called into the din.

Victor led her down the hall in the midst of a hungry mob, toward the source of the tantalizing aroma.

Caroline had expected vegetarian food. She was wrong. Baked chicken, fragrant with citrus and cilantro, lay piled on a platter in the center of a long, rough-hewn table covered in a cloth printed with a sunburst pattern. Spanish rice, beans, tortillas, a bowl of cut tomatoes, and salsas in a variety of colors also crowded the fabric, nearly obliterating the pattern.

She dug into the food with delight. It tasted delicious, and her belly rumbled and ached, begging her to hurry.

All around her people laughed and chatted, some in English, some in Spanish, and some in a perplexing combination of the two.

Bilingualism and *code-switching*, she amended her earlier research topic. *How cool. I wonder if they'd let me study their interactions... or just hang out again... often. This is so noisy and boisterous compared to family gatherings at the Jones home.* Idle chitchat, good-natured banter, and even some edgy teasing circulated around the table. Caroline couldn't help but smile.

Caroline took a bite of her beans. Not the ubiquitous refried variety, these sat in little bowls, bathed in broth in which chunks of savory bacon floated. The complex flavors burst on her tongue until she accidentally bit into a large chunk of jalapeño pepper. It burned. She sipped her tea hoping no one would notice, but the burn intensified until her eyes watered. She waved her hand in front of her mouth.

"Did you get something hot?" Victor asked her, setting down the chicken leg he'd been chomping.

"Uh-huh."

"Iced tea won't help. It just spreads the heat around. Here, eat this." He pressed a warm handmade tortilla into her hand.

She took a bite. The bread did cool the burning a little, at least in her mouth, but her stomach didn't appreciate the pepper either. The churning returned full-force. She swallowed hard.

"Caroline?" Sam said to call her attention.

She turned. "Ms. Johnston?"

"Call me Sam," the older woman replied, tucking a strand of burnished hair behind her ear. "I'm glad you came tonight."

Caroline smiled, trying to look friendly as she struggled to ignore the burn in her belly. "Of course. I'm glad to be invited."

Sam leaned forward conspiratorially. "Victor's never brought a woman to meet the family before. I thought he might choose to remain single. When he told us, years ago, that he was in love with his English professor, I didn't know what to think. I figured it was his way of saying a relationship wasn't part of his plans. While an unpartnered life is a valid choice, I never thought that was truly what he wanted. I'm glad that you're with him now."

Caroline smiled and tried to swallow. The burn seemed to be spreading upward into her throat, but she made herself answer anyway. "Why not? Now that he's not my student anymore, I can see him for what he really is... a wonderful man. I simply adore him." *I'm gushing, though I doubt Sam will mind. And it takes my mind off the heartburn… somewhat.*

The woman beamed. "Good. It takes a special kind of woman to appreciate someone so shy. It's really great though. When you know your man has overcome such a powerful compulsion to be silent and has done it for you, well, that's a really special thing."

"It is," Caroline agreed, swallowing a burp, "but Victor's never been that shy with me."

"I guess he trusts you." Sam's smile crinkled her eyes the same way Victor's did.

Caroline couldn't help smiling back. "I'm glad of that. I know we haven't been together long, but I can really see him as the kind of man I'd like to marry."

Sam sighed. "So you're a traditional type. He'd probably be happy to do it too. I won't lie to you; I don't think much of marriage. You don't need a piece of paper from the government to give you permission to love someone. It's not their business. Just an excuse to meddle and extract fees."

"I understand your opinion," Caroline said carefully, wanting to make her point without offending, "but I don't really agree. I see marriage as a statement about your feelings. Like, I love this man and I want everyone to know it. I've chosen him and I'm proud of him."

Sam grinned. "Well, that's not a bad thing. Victor deserves that."

"He does. Um, excuse me a moment." Caroline jumped up from the table and hurried down the hallway, in urgent search of a bathroom. She found one along the right-hand wall. Closing the door and locking it, she fell to her knees beside the toilet. The unwanted jalapeño proved too much for her pregnant stomach, and she expelled it, along with the rest of the food she'd gobbled. *I had expected this, but not at Victor's birthday party. How embarrassing.*

Caroline clutched the cool porcelain with both hands

as her body attempted to turn itself inside out. Once the spasms finally passed, she dragged herself unsteadily to her feet, took a deep breath and wiped her lips with the back of her hand.

She washed her hands and splashed cool water on her face before she opened the door.

Sam stood outside. "Are you all right, Caroline?" she asked, eyes filled with concern.

"Yes," Caroline replied weakly. The aroma of roasted chicken, which had a few moments ago smelled so appealing, assaulted her. She gagged again and swallowed hard, wiping away a ribbon of saliva from her lower lip.

"Come on." Taking her elbow, Sam led her through the house to a room near the back. What had once been a kitchenette now appeared to have become her studio, as art supplies lay in messy piles on a blue laminate counter and a wooden work table. Clay sculpting tools lay in a white porcelain sink, both heavily stained with paint.

The coolness of the room refreshed Caroline's sweaty face. The pleasant scent of incense and clay soothed her lingering nausea. She closed her eyes and breathed deeply, trying to regain control of herself.

Sam pulled a plastic cup from the cabinet and filled it from a water dispenser in the corner. She handed the drink to Caroline, who sipped it gratefully, still terribly embarrassed.

"I can remember what that's like," Sam said. "Horrible isn't it? There's a reason I only have one child."

"Is it that obvious?" Caroline's cheeks heated, even as she laid her hand on her belly, unconsciously confirming the woman's guess.

Sam grinned indulgently. "Uh-huh. I mean, you kind of gave yourself away. You told me you're not doing alcohol right now, and I just found you retching in the bathroom. How far along are you?"

"I'm not sure," Caroline admitted. She swirled a

mouthful of water in her mouth. "I just found out, but probably only a couple of weeks. It can't have been long."

Sam beamed. "Victor must be ecstatic."

Caroline took another cautious swallow of the water. For the moment, it seemed inclined to stay put. "Yes. I am too."

"No wonder you two are talking about marriage. He always was such a traditional boy, despite my best efforts." Sam pursed her lips.

She's happy about the baby, but not about the idea of marriage, just as Victor told me. How interesting. She really isn't like any mother I've ever known. "He's not, you know." Caroline's knees still felt none too steady. She pulled a chair out from the table and sank into it.

The older woman's eyebrows shot up. "How so?"

Okay, time to go for broke. If Victor described her correctly, this should impress her. "What would you say if I told you that your 'traditional boy' once found his English professor—an older woman by the way—crying because she thought she would never be able to have a baby? What if I told you that he offered to give her one right then and there, with or without a relationship?"

"Is that what happened?" Sam's eyebrows shot so high, she creased her forehead like a plowed field. She leaned against the counter as though in shock.

"Yes." Caroline touched the cool cup to her burning face. *This is an awkward conversation to have with a near-total stranger. I hope it pays off.*

Wow. I'm impressed." Then Sam's face changed. "I'm not really surprised though. He's made that kind of donation before. I'm sorry to say this, and please don't take offense, but I don't like it much. I can't imagine something as vital as a baby coming from such a cold, clinical procedure."

Cold and clinical? Caroline's cheeks heated as memories of Victor's passionate lovemaking swirled in her mind. "I don't know anything about that. Victor made it pretty clear that where I was concerned, only the natural fertilization method would do." She blurted, blushing hotter. "Nothing cold or clinical about it."

Sam grinned. "Ah, that's good. So the pregnancy came before the relationship? What caused you two to get together then?"

"They happened at the same time," Caroline admitted, feeling strengthened by Sam's approval. "Once I got past the idea of Victor as a student, I wanted him as much as I wanted a baby. Now I have both. I'm so terribly lucky." And she felt it too. At least, until another wave of nausea rolled up. Caroline gagged but hid it behind a swallow of water.

Sam continued, not noticing. "I'm glad for you then." She eyed Caroline closely. "There's no way you're older than Victor though. He's thirty-one, you know."

"Yes, I know. I'm thirty-three."

Sam blinked, scrutinizing her even more closely. Her gaze traced over Caroline's features with the sharpness of a sculptor's tool. "Really? My goodness, you look younger."

"Thank you." Caroline smiled weakly and broke eye contact as shyness overtook her. She stared into her water and noticing the cup had little blue flowers on it.

Silence fell as the two women considered each other, Sam smiling, Caroline feeling warmed by the approval of the woman she knew had the ability to cause trouble for her and Victor, if she wanted. *Looks like she likes me so far.*

"Caroline, I have something to give you," Sam said after a few moments.

Caroline inhaled deeply and noted with relief that her nausea had mostly passed. Only a faint burn remained. "Sure, okay."

Sam opened a drawer below the counter and pulled

out… something. She beckoned to Caroline, who rose unsteadily and crossed the room. Taking her hand, Sam tucked into it a bracelet made of crocheted gold wire, threaded with pink and green beads arranged into little flowers. Long dangling earrings in a matching pattern completed the set.

"These are beautiful!" Caroline exclaimed. "Thank you." She wrapped the bracelet around her wrist and hung the earrings from her ears. *I bet, with my short hair, the dangling flowers look terrific.*

"You're welcome, Caroline. I'm glad you and Victor are together." Suddenly Sam's expression turned fierce. "You take good care of my boy, Caroline. He hasn't had the easiest time in the romance department. Don't you dare lead him on like that other one did."

Caroline raised her eyes from the bracelet. "No, I swear. I'm not leading him on. I love him."

Sam shook her head with a wry smile. "Maternal instincts. You'll understand soon enough."

Maternal instincts. How perfect is that? I'm a mother now. She touched her belly in wonder. "I'm sure."

Clearly misunderstanding the gesture, Sam said, "How's your stomach, honey? Still queasy?"

"Not right now," Caroline replied, smiling.

Warm arms slid around Caroline from behind. "Here you are." Victor's breath felt warm against her ear. "I couldn't find you."

"She needed a moment," Sam said blandly. "The morning sickness got to her."

His arms stiffened. "Oh, are you okay?"

"I'm fine," Caroline replied. "I'd better watch out for those hot peppers though. They sure don't like me."

"They're a little much for the typical Midwestern palate." Victor laid his hand on Caroline's belly. "So you told her, did you?"

"I didn't have to," Caroline admitted, her cheeks heating. "She found me in the bathroom while I was parting ways with the jalapeño. I guess she figured it out."

Victor kissed her cheek.

"I'm awfully proud of you, Victor," Sam said, her eyes glowing. "You chose well. She's a treasure."

"I know it," he answered, and the warmth in his voice sent tingles from Caroline's scalp to the tips of her toes. "It's been wonderful. I knew if I could just convince her to see me as something other than a student, it would be amazing."

"No, Victor," Caroline said, suddenly feeling equally intense. She reached up and laid her hand on his cheek. "You're amazing. I love you."

He touched his lips to her temple.

"Well," said Sam, beaming, "if you're sure you're all right, Caroline, we should probably get back to the party. The guest of honor has candles to blow out and cake to eat."

Caroline thought about cake and shuddered. "This is the strangest sensation."

"Just about the time you get used to it, it will change," Sam replied in a less than reassuring way.

"No doubt," Caroline agreed wryly.

They headed back to the party.

Caroline regarded the *tres leches* cake Victor's Aunt Lupita had made. The knife sank in and sweetened condensed milk oozed from it. Her mouth watered at the sight. Despite her previous revulsion, she devoured a large slice.

Being pregnant is proving to be very weird.

CHAPTER 6

*M*onday morning, Caroline graded the research papers. Her mind wandered as she flagged faulty citations and weak parallelism.

Freshman composition isn't my favorite class to teach, she admitted to herself in the privacy of her mind, *but since Sheridan Murphy got hired as a full-time lecturer two years ago, I thankfully only have one section per semester. Sheridan, for whatever reason, loves that class. I suppose she enjoys preparing her students for Michael since he appreciates her success so much.*

She paused, her gaze straying to the portraits of the Brownings hanging on her wall. They brought her mind around to romance. *After pursuing him for several years, Michael finally succumbed to the lures of his beautiful former student and she moved in with him. They're a nice couple and I'm glad for them.*

I wonder how Michael reconciled his staunch Catholic faith with cohabitation. I suppose sometimes rules have to be broken. I can relate. Coming home each night to Victor's warmth and passion in my bed is a joy I don't even want to imagine giving up. Since we found out about the pregnancy, he seems to desire me even more.

Her belly churned, reminding her of the downside. Her morning sickness, having begun so suddenly, had taken on a life of its own. No advice, no suggestion, no remedy could soothe it. She vomited frequently, even at work, which left her as miserable as she was ecstatic. *I hope it passes soon. Meanwhile, I should pay attention to what I'm doing.*

She glanced down at the stack of documents and wrote in a missing comma in green pen before her mind wandered again.

Next week, between administering finals, I'll go to the doctor for a checkup. Unfortunately, Victor has an exam in his mechanical engineering class and won't be able to attend with me. Hopefully, as Sophie will be on her lunch break at the daycare, she'll be able to lend moral support. I'll ask her tonight.

She grinned. *I can't wait for the girls to meet Victor. Maggie says she's bringing Selene too. I suppose the company will be more fun than the drinks, as almost half of the group is pregnant and limited to tea or lemonade.* The thought of the acidic citrus beverage turned Caroline's stomach and she had to swallow hard several times.

Fishing in her purse, she pulled out a sugar-free mint, hoping it would help. "Grade the papers, Dr. Jones," she grumbled aloud to herself. Forcing her mind back to her work once again, she flipped the graded paper to the back of the pile and frowned to see Nick's name on the next one.

Even a quick glance at the first page revealed a number of typos that the simplest spell checker would have caught. She leafed through, slightly mollified by the sight of embedded citations, sloppy and poorly formatted, but present. Then she turned to the back.

No works cited page.

She ground her teeth. *I warned the class repeatedly about this. I also warned Nick one on one, several times. He ignored me. Damned kid.*

The rubric clearly stated that the citations would form one-third of the grade for this paper. The paper counted for one-quarter of the class grade. To ensure success, they had completed their works cited pages in class, under her supervision. He had been a no-show that entire week.

This is a disaster. Even with the embedded citations, he will be unlikely to get a 70. If he fails this class, he'll be on academic probation, and that means he won't be able to participate in sports in the spring semester. He should have listened.

She graded the paper, carefully following her rubric to the letter. Being as generous as possible, she was still only able to mark the paper with a 60. Barely a D. Added to the rest of his poor work this semester, his semester average going into the final would be a 61.

As though her thoughts had summoned him, Nick sauntered into the room. "Hello, Dr. Jones. Did you grade my paper?"

Caroline nailed him with a disapproving glare. "Yes. Just what the hell kind of paper was that? Where was your works cited page?"

He spread his arms and played dumb. "I cited. I did just what you said. I put them in the paper."

"Yes, I saw that," she replied dryly, "but you also needed a works cited page."

"What for?" he demanded, blinking in wide-eyed stupidity.

You don't fool me, twerp. You knew better, and you intentionally tried to get away with it. "Because that's how it's done," Caroline told him dryly. A throbbing in her temple revealed the anger she tried to squash down in order to seem more professional. "I told you that, no exceptions."

He smirked, clearly still not admitting to understanding the seriousness of what he had done. "Okay, so then what did I get, a C?"

You think you can ignore the syllabus, my explicit instructions and every rule of college writing and still sneak out a pass? You have another think coming, mister. "You got a D, and you're darn lucky for that," she replied, teeth grinding in frustration.

Nick's dopey expression dissolved into one of astonishment, and then anger. "You can't do that." He leaned his hands on the desk, crowding into her space.

She didn't back up, but lifted her chin, meeting his eyes without flinching. "I can."

"But I can't get another D!" His voice rose in volume.

Caroline kept her own tone calm and cool. "Well, Nick, that's your best option at this point. Even if you ace the final, your class average will still be in the 60s."

Nick's temper snapped. He pointed a finger directly into her face. "Now listen here, you little bitch, I'm not going to be on academic probation because of you."

"No," she agreed, unintimidated, "you're going to be on academic probation because of *you*."

His blue eyes narrowed to threatening little slits. "No, I'm not. Let me explain this to you. You're going to go and change that D to a C right now. The baseball team needs me, and what about football in the fall? You're not going to mess that up."

Caroline scoffed. "Dream on, Nick. In my class, you get the grade you earn."

His expression changed, turned from fury to... something else, something sly and nauseating. "Are you sure about that? What can I do to earn a few extra points? I know I can give it to you better than that Mexican. I got it where it counts... little teacher." He reached for her while gesturing with his pelvis.

She jerked back. His sick imitation of Victor's sweet endearment nauseated her. In her fury, her voice dropped to an icy hiss. "Don't you *ever* say that to me again. You will address me as Dr. Jones, and you will watch what you say to me or you'll have worse than a D to deal with."

Nick's expression turned furious.

Caroline became starkly aware of his overwhelming size—well over a foot taller than her—muscular and athletic.

No, I won't waver. I have the authority here and I will not be intimidated. She glared at the young man.

Seeming to realize his tactic wasn't working, he snarled, "You're going to be sorry you messed with me, *Doctor* Jones. I know what you're doing. You fix my grade right now, and I won't go to the dean about your little affair. I'm sure she'd be thrilled to know you're screwing a student."

Caroline's rage boiled over. "Are you threatening me? I haven't done anything wrong, and your accusation won't save you. Last chance. Get out of here. Go study for your final or it's going to be an F."

He glared another moment, making it clear he didn't respect her authority. Then he cracked his knuckles, turned on his heel and stomped out, sneakers squeaking on the tile.

She shook her head. *That was, without a doubt, the worst confrontation I've ever had with a student.*

Her nausea rose again, and the mint did nothing to quell it. Resignedly, she hurried into the ladies' room across the hall and succumbed to morning sickness yet again.

~

Later that afternoon, the chair of the English department, Dr. Howard Miller, called Caroline to his office.

What an unwelcoming room, she thought, looking through the open door. The desk, though mahogany, stood stark and undecorated, housing only the computer, a set of black plastic stacking trays and an oversized calendar. Two broad oak chairs in a pale stain that clashed with the darkness of the desk had been placed across from the professor's second-hand, black leather office chair.

Cheap metal bookshelves ringed the walls, but no cheerful novels added color. Only heavy old textbooks lent their musty breath to the lifeless space. The window had white plastic blinds, but no curtains.

She knocked on the open door.

He glanced up, the fluorescent light flashing on the top of his shiny bald head. His ring of overlong white hair bounced with the movement. He waved her into a seat. "Caroline," he began without preamble, "I've just received a very disturbing phone call from Dr. Perry."

"Oh? What did she have to say?" Caroline asked, though she had a feeling she knew why the Dean of the College of Humanities might have called her department chair.

"Dr. Perry said a student came to see her earlier today claiming his teacher had been grading him unfairly," Dr. Miller intoned, his expression daring her to react.

"Ah, yes. That would be Nicholas Randall, wouldn't it?" she asked calmly.

He lowered his eyebrows. "Yes."

"Dr. Miller," Caroline explained, "Nick has made some very questionable choices this semester. The last straw was turning in his research paper without a works cited page. He's going to get a D even if he aces his final. It's the best I can do."

"From what he told Dr. Perry, he's not the only one who's been making questionable choices."

Caroline waited in silence.

Dr. Miller continued. "Of course, I don't want to believe it could be true, but Mr. Randall is of the opinion that you are involved in an intimate relationship with a senior engineering major named Victor Martinez, and that the two of you, in fact, live together."

She tried not to grind her teeth. *That little jackass. How dare he?* "And?"

He lowered his eyebrows even further in consternation. The bushy salt and pepper hairs threatened to obscure his squinty eyes altogether. "Is it true?"

"Yes," she admitted, "but I fail to see how it's relevant."

Dr. Miller threw his hands in the air. "Caroline, it makes the whole department look bad. Not to mention that it calls into question your professionalism."

"I can't imagine how."

"Mr. Martinez is a student," he drawled in a sarcastic tone, as though it were obvious.

"He's not *my* student," Caroline reminded her supervisor.

"But he used to be, isn't that true?"

"Over a year ago!" Caroline protested.

"Don't you think it's still a little… improper?" Dr. Miller insisted.

"No!" she exclaimed. "No more than any of my unmarried colleagues having close relationships with another adult. I have no academic authority over Victor. He's not in my class. University policy on this is clear."

Dr. Miller pressed his fingertips to his shiny forehead. "Damn it, Caroline, you're a professor. You can't just take in this young man and keep him like a pet."

"I'm not," she shot back. "And he's not that young. We're nearly the same age. He's more than capable of making his own decisions. I'm not taking advantage."

"Well, you've certainly set yourself up to be questioned. Nicholas is demanding to have his essay graded by someone else."

She shrugged. "Let him. I doubt it will improve his score."

"But he's called your entire grading policy into question. There's going to be an investigation of your impartiality."

"Let them look," she hissed. "I've never graded a student unfairly."

"Not even Victor?" He made quotation marks in the air with his fingers as he spoke her boyfriend's name.

She forced herself to inhale deeply and slowly. "No. We weren't involved then. I graded his work the same as anyone else's. I would have regardless."

Thankfully, he took a deep breath and matched her painfully neutral tone. "It's going to be hard for you to prove that."

Caroline took a deep breath. "What do I need to do?"

"I'll get back to you about that, once the Dean and I have conferred in person. May I give you one suggestion though?"

Caroline waited—holding her breath—for the other shoe to drop.

"Break things off with your young man. It doesn't do you any good professionally to be involved with him."

"I can't do that. I won't," she told him, her lip and voice wavering against her will.

"Why not?"

"Because I'm in love with Victor, and because…" she sucked in air and swallowed a gag, "because I'm pregnant with his baby."

Dr. Miller promptly went to pieces again. His head turned so red it resembled a tomato. A vein throbbed in his temple. "Oh my God, Caroline! Are you insane? Why would you do such a thing?"

She refused to go there with him. "It's not anyone's business. I'm not breaking any rules. Victor is of age. Besides, this is hardly unprecedented in our department."

"What do you mean?" His jaw began to twitch.

"Well look at Michael and Sheridan. They live together, and she was his student for *six years*. Everyone knows they've been in love forever, but they claim not to have acted on it until this semester. And what about Davontay? He's dating an English major, for crying out loud. What I'm doing is not worse than either of those things. It's just another example of a relationship between two consenting adults." She narrowed her eyes. "Is this because I'm a woman and Michael and Davontay are men?"

The oblique reference to sexism settled the older professor instantly. They both knew he couldn't afford that kind of accusation. "No. It's because you are the one whose integrity has been called into question. As for Michael, he's such a tough professor no one would dare question him. I'll speak to Davontay. He's asking for trouble with that one. But you're not off the hook, Caroline. I think this affair is ill-advised and will lead to trouble. Prepare yourself and your young man to answer some serious questions. And don't forget you're up for tenure this year. This isn't going to look good."

Suddenly, Caroline felt cold. Her fingertips tingled and her lips went numb. "So my years of service, my excellent student evaluations, my publications, my membership on committees and my recruitment efforts mean nothing because I've chosen to have a personal relationship?" Though she held it in, the urge to weep welled up in her.

"Because you've chosen to sleep with a student."

His icy tone settled like lead in the pit of her stomach. "Are you going to reject my tenure?" she asked in a voice far steadier than she would have believed possible, giving her roiling insides.

"No," he admitted. "That's not solely my decision to make, but this incident will certainly be included in your file. It could make a difference to the committee, depending on how they view such... proceedings."

She steeled herself again. "I'm sorry to hear that, but I'm still not changing anything. I need to be with Victor."

Dr. Miller sighed heavily. "Well, you've made your position very clear. I hope it doesn't come back to haunt you." He dismissed her with a wave of one hand.

Nervous discomfort churn in Caroline's guts as she walked away. *When I counted the cost of this pregnancy, I figured on diapers, cute little clothes, soccer team and ballet lessons, but I never thought it would threaten my career. How can I provide for a baby without my job?*

She shuddered, eyes burning with more than hormones. *I love it here. I've invested six years in this position. Have I thrown it all away on a whim? Dear Lord, what have I done?*

She sniffled, and, finding herself back in her office, sank into her chair in exhaustion. A frisson of nausea fluttered through her. Though the sensation felt unpleasant, it reminded her of her goal. *There are other schools. There are other jobs. This is your child. That will now and forever after take precedence.*

Not knowing what to do or how to feel, she tried to suppress her confusion, but with little success. *Good luck, kiddos. Your teacher is not having a good day.* Sighing, she grasped the handful of essays and forced her mind away from both babies and threats and tried with all her might to focus on work. *At least I still know how to do this, even if everything else has stopped making sense.*

~

That evening, when Caroline walked into her favorite restaurant, hand-in-hand with her beloved, she gripped his fingers as though he were her lifeline. She led him to their usual booth, on time for once, and ordered iced tea from the waiter who stood nearby. Victor eyed the ladies, and she wondered what he saw as he asked for the same drink as her. The group arrayed around the table seemed mostly as familiar to her as her own face

117

SIMONE BEAUDELAIRE

in the mirror, but apart from Maggie, her shy boyfriend knew none of them.

"Hi, everyone," Caroline exclaimed, waving to her friends.

"Hi," the other ladies chorused. Caroline regarded the circle of friends. *Sophie brought her kids this time. Nice. Maybe without Jessica and her dirty comments, Sophie feels better about having them here.* She smiled at nine-year-old Andie, who stared at her mom's cell phone with intense concentration, and two-year-old Alex, who perched on Sophie's lap, thumb in mouth.

Tonight, Sophie glowed with happiness. Alex and Andie also lit up the table with full-lipped grins. The three of them matched perfectly, with medium olive skin, dark brown hair and brown eyes. Sophie's Italian ancestry clearly showed in her offspring.

I wonder if my baby will have the look of Victor's Mexican heritage. That would be nice. For a moment, her attention strayed to the tiny, bean-sized person currently occupying space in her belly. She pictured tan skin and dark eyes, and her heart melted. Then, pulling herself together, she slid into the booth next to her friends.

This time, as promised, Maggie had brought Selene with her. Caroline had met Maggie's best friend—now her stepmother—before. She had joined them a few times in the past, but then she had been painfully thin and shy. Now she had new confidence; that of a woman who knows she is loved. Her seven-month belly swelled attractively under her maternity shirt; her wedding ring sparkled on her finger.

"Hello, Selene," Caroline greeted the other woman politely, breaking the ice. "I'm glad you decided to join us. Congratulations on your wedding, by the way."

"Thank you," the blond replied in a soft, but no longer quite so timid voice, "I'm glad to be here. I'm sorry, but that other friend of yours made me so uncomfortable, I just couldn't come unless she was gone. She never did have your best interests at heart, you know."

"I know that now." *But how odd that Selene, a virtual stranger, also does.* "How did you realize it?"

"Selene is one of the most intuitive people you will ever meet," Maggie said. "If she tells you something, you should always listen."

Selene gave Maggie a speaking look Caroline could not interpret.

Rather than asking probing questions, she proceeded to introductions. "This is Victor, my boyfriend. Victor, this is Sophie. You already know Maggie, of course, and Selene is Maggie's best friend."

"Pleased to meet you, ladies," Victor said softly. He took a sip of his iced tea and his arm tightened around Caroline's back.

"So what are the announcements this week?" Caroline asked.

"I just heard from Brett," Sophie said. "His deployment is scheduled to end in two weeks. Lord and military willing, he should be home to stay this time. I'm keeping my fingers crossed."

"That's great," Caroline told her friend.

"And, you'll be glad to know, I've finally set a date. I hope to see all of you at our wedding in May." She beamed as everyone nodded. "Who's next?"

"I don't have news," Selene said. "You can clearly see what I've been up to lately." She patted her belly with her left hand, and her wedding ring flashed.

"So, Caroline," Sophie continued, "What's new with you?"

"Everything, I guess." She leaned her cheek on Victor's shoulder. "My whole life is changing. I'm so excited I could just burst."

"Please, not at the table." Selene's quip wasn't that funny, but everyone laughed anyway.

Caroline continued. "I don't know if you are all

SIMONE BEAUDELAIRE

aware, but Victor and I are expecting a baby. This was intentional and we're both very happy about it."

"So you got everything you wanted, did you?" Sophie asked her friend, raising one eyebrow.

"So far everything is looking good." She smiled, but worries about her work situation tempered its brilliance.

"Have you been to the doctor yet?" Maggie asked.

"I have an appointment on Monday at one. Sophie, is there any way you can come with me?"

Sophie lit up like the candle in the middle of the table. "I would love to."

They looked around at one another, casting about for another topic of conversation.

Selene sighed with relief as the waiter approached to take their order. Her audible exhalation gave Maggie the giggles and earned a stern stare from her stepmother as they requested burgers, sandwiches and French fries. At last, Selene cleared her throat and asked, "So, Victor, what do you do?"

He smiled, tension radiating up his spine, but took a deep breath and answered her question. "I'm a senior majoring in engineering."

Sophie gave him an appraising look, which he caught and responded to.

"I was in the military for several years, so I may be a bit behind the typical timetable, but I figure... I'm going to get older whether I go to school or not, so I might as well keep after it. What about you?"

Selene blinked, realizing she was being addressed. "Oh, I work for the police department."

Caroline had to suppress a giggle at his shell-shocked reaction, imagining the tiny, pregnant blond driving a squad car.

"Selene has a gift for interrogations," Maggie added. "They keep her around the station for when they have particularly tricky suspects to question."

120

Selene nodded in agreement and the conversation stalled again.

This is rough. Hopefully, we can all get over the hurdle soon, Caroline thought, *but at least no one is being mean, just shy and uncomfortable.*

About half an hour later, Caroline realized she needed the restroom, though thankfully not due to overwhelming nausea.

"Excuse me, everyone," she said, rising.

"Are you all right?" Victor stared into her face, searching for signs of a problem.

"Yes, I'm fine," she told him. Leaning in close, she whispered. "Nature calls. Nothing to worry about, honey."

He grinned. "That's good." Then he drew her down and kissed her cheek.

She beamed. Blushing with happiness, she made her way through the tan carpeted room past a crowd of rowdy undergraduates who gulped beer and cheered at the game on the east-facing television. They whistled as she went by.

She couldn't help but snort. *I'm out of your league and your age group, boys.* Rolling her eyes, she ducked behind the bathroom door and out of sight.

The scent of bleach elicited a gag. Holding her nose with one hand, she managed to suppress the nausea before it could fully develop. While she was occupied in one of the stalls, the door opened and closed.

Caroline emerged and approached the sink to wash her hands with a squirt of pinkish soap that smelled appealingly like almond extract. The sweet aroma banished the gagging sensation arising from the stench of the bleach. She shook her head. *This scent revulsion thing is beyond annoying.*

The stall in the corner opened and Selene emerged. Standing, the slender woman had begun to look uncomfortably heavy, her no-nonsense policewoman walk transforming into a waddle. She crossed the room to the sink and washed her hands sink next to Caroline.

"I know it's not considered polite," Caroline told her as they threw their paper towels in the trash, "but your baby bump really is adorable."

Selene beamed. "Thank you. I think some of the rules about what's polite are just silly. Here. He's kicking. Want to feel?"

Caroline extended her hand.

Selene hesitated, then grasped it and pressed it to her belly.

How weird. She offered to let me feel it and then held back. But the sensation Caroline experienced drove the thought from her mind. A heavy thump, followed by what could only be a foot pushed against her hand. "Oh, wow, Selene. He's strong." Caroline exclaimed.

"He is. I can't imagine what he's going to be doing in there two months from now. I feel like I'm going to fall over already." She couched the complaint in a grin. "Um, Caroline?"

"Yes?"

"Can I tell you something?" Selene looked worried, her green eyes clouded, the corners tight.

"Sure."

"This is going to sound weird, but... don't feel bad about ending your friendship with Jessica."

Caroline lowered her eyebrows at Selene. "I don't."

"Okay," Selene didn't look convinced, but she accepted the comment, nonetheless. "I'm not kidding that she didn't have your best interests at heart. A lot of the trouble you've run into since college was because of her. She's always been jealous of you, and that's why she tried to bring you down. It was deliberate."

Caroline looked at Selene, knowing her expression mirrored the confusion she felt.

"I know," Selene added with a wry twist of the lips.

"I'm freaky weird. But I know what I'm telling you. You haven't lost a friend. Not at all."

Well then. I mean, what she's saying could be right, never mind that she couldn't possibly know anything about it. Shaking her head, Caroline replied, "Okay, Selene, thank you." Her stomach gurgled with a new sensation. "Come on, let's go back. I don't know about you, but I'm starving. It's so weird. A minute ago I thought I was full. Isn't pregnancy bizarre?"

"Oh yeah." Selene nodded, clearly just as glad to change the subject, "I'm always hungry these days. This little boy has a huge appetite."

They walked back out to the dining room together. *I'm not sure what that conversation was about, but Selene sounded sincere, and her words certainly rang true. In a strange way, it was comforting to hear.*

～

Back at home in bed, Caroline snuggled close to Victor. His arms around her felt so good, especially as the smell of food on her clothing had made her so nauseous that upon entering the house she had barely made it to the bathroom. Now, teeth brushed and just where she wanted to be, she felt a bit better. *It doesn't matter that I've been with this man only since Thanksgiving, not quite a month. This is the realest connection I've ever felt.* Then she recalled the Nick Randall situation and tension crept her spine.

"Little teacher, you're tight as a spring," Victor commented, rubbing her back with one hand. "What's wrong?"

"Nothing." She didn't want to worry him, so she tried to suppress the desire to pour out the whole story.

He petted her hair. "I can feel it in every muscle of your body. Tell me."

She sighed. "There's a little... situation going on at work, and it's making me nervous."

"What's that?" he pressed.

Damn, I guess I can't avoid Victor's urge to share my troubles with me. "Do you remember when you came to my office and reminded me about your mother's invitation to dinner?"

"Yeah, why?"

"We were overheard."

Victor's eyebrows drew together. "We were?"

"Yes, by a student of mine. You might recall that he was arguing with me about his research paper."

She saw realization dawning in his eyes. "Ah yes. How do you know he heard us?"

"He called me little teacher." She shuddered. "He knew you were a student and that we live together. He also threatened to turn us in to the dean if I didn't raise his grade."

"Oh." Victor thought for a moment. "Did he do that?"

Caroline frowned. "Yes."

Victor's expression darkened. "And?"

"Well, he wants someone else to grade his paper. That's not going to get him very far, but my department chair is pretty pissed at me," she admitted, frowning.

"Why?"

"He thinks our relationship makes the department look bad."

Victor made a face. "How?"

Caroline rolled her eyes. "I'm not sure, but he's really worried about it. I think in the near future they may be taking a closer look at the papers you wrote in my class, just to be sure I didn't unfairly elevate your grade because of our relationship."

"We didn't have a relationship then," he reminded her.

"I told Dr. Miller that, but he didn't believe me."

Caroline exhaled a sigh. *I wish people would mind their own business... and it's a sad day when a professor has to defend herself against a student with such an obvious reason to cause trouble.*

Victor's face took on the expression she knew so well, the one that meant all the gears in his head were turning. "Well, I still have everything. They can certainly look. I know you didn't do that. You were really tough."

"You asked me to be," she pointed out.

His grin looked strained, which caused a further pang in her already burdened heart. *Was this all a mistake then? Is that even possible?*

"It wasn't a criticism, Caroline. I did ask that. Okay, so worst-case scenario, what could happen? They can't fire you for this, can they? You didn't break any rules."

"No," she replied. "I've looked up the university policy on professors dating students. We're fine. The problem is, I'm up for tenure this year. I've been working towards it for six years. If I don't get it, I'm basically through here. I might be able to work year to year as a lecturer, but a full-time permanent position is out. It's not being fired, but it amounts to the same thing. I'm under contract until the end of spring semester, but after that, I might just be out. Dr. Miller mentioned that this... situation might make the difference between being accepted and rejected for tenure."

"Oh God, Caroline, I'm so sorry." He cupped her cheeks in his hands. "I didn't want to ruin your career, only to make you happy."

"You have made me happy," she told him fiercely, wrapping her arms around his chest. "I've never been happy like this. I love you, and I'm overjoyed to be pregnant with your baby. None of that is the university's business." Her thoughts turned bleak. "But what will we do if I lose my job?"

He paused to consider again.

Engineers solve problems, and Victor has that skill in spades. When did he ever fail to find an angle, explore it and defend it? He's a champion, Caroline reminded herself.

"You're sure they have to keep you through the spring?"

"Yes. It would be almost unheard of to fire a professor mid-semester unless I'd broken the law. The spring semester schedule is made already, so it would be a huge hassle to replace me, especially in my senior and graduate-level courses. And I'm under contract until May regardless. Basically, trying to get rid of me during this academic year would be more trouble than it's worth. They're stuck with me until summer."

"Well, that's when I graduate. I'm going to start networking ASAP. I don't think you're going to want so many overtime hours next fall anyway, are you? Not since you'll be having a baby in the middle of summer, so I need a job regardless. Don't fret, Caroline. I'll be able to provide for our family by then, even if you're… if you take a bit of time off from work to be with our baby while you… look for a new position."

It was the solution she'd wanted but not quite dared hope for. Tension released in Caroline's shoulders, leaving her breathless. "I'm so thankful for you, Victor. Can I show you how thankful I am?" she asked impishly.

His wicked, full-lipped grin returned to its former sparkle, heating her instantly to nuclear. "I would love it if you would."

CHAPTER 7

The following Monday, final exams began, starting with Nick's class. He arrived half an hour late, an unpleasant expression on his chiseled face.

Caroline ignored him. Her stomach concerned her far more than that lazy jock.

The exam lingered forever, while Caroline swallowed hard and ate mints to suppress a few unpleasant gagging sensations. When it finally ended, she bid a relieved goodbye to her students and crossed campus to the daycare to collect Sophie for the doctor's appointment. As she walked into the building, she ran into Alyssa Miller, the former student she had mentioned to Victor recently.

"Hi, Alyssa," she greeted the slender strawberry blonde in the hallway, noting in passing that a mural of Sesame Street characters had been painted on the walls. *What a cheerful place. I guess if I don't lose my job, my baby will spend some time here.*

"Dr. Jones, how are you?" The girl smiled, which did unpleasant things to the taut, undernourished flesh of her cheeks.

"Pretty good," Caroline replied, trying not to stare. "What about you?"

"Oh, I just keep doing my best." Alyssa made a

brave face, but the sorrow in her eyes shone bright as tears. She leaned against the wall as though not certain of her strength.

"Let me know if there's anything I can do. I worry about you, you know," Caroline told her bluntly. "Stop by and say hello sometimes."

"I'll do that." Alyssa entered the nursery and scooped up her tiny, auburn-haired son, kissing him on the cheek.

Caroline's heart clenched at the sight. She pressed her hand consideringly to her belly. *I can't wait to meet you, my little one.*

Knocking on the window, she got the attention of her closest friend. Sophie hurried out of the daycare, shouting instructions over her shoulder to the undergraduates who sat on the floor playing patty cake with a group of fascinated toddlers.

"They are so cute," Caroline commented.

Sophie grinned. "I should say something realistic, like how they drive me crazy, shouldn't I? But I won't. I love kids."

They made their way down the hallway. Caroline, who for once felt great, quipped, "Then it's a good thing you and Brett are finally tying the knot. Am I right that you want one of those big Italian families, not just two kids?"

Sophie beamed. "I could manage a couple more, I think. What about you? Now that you have a baby-daddy to help you out, what are your plans?"

Caroline shrugged and then shivered as they pushed open the door and a blast of frozen wind stung her. "I'm happy to have one on the way." She patted her belly through her thick coat. "After that, who knows? It may be that this is it. Time will tell."

Sophie rolled her eyes. "Thirty-five isn't an expiration date, you know. You probably could try again later."

"I might," Caroline concurred. "But first things first. How bad is this going to be?"

"Better practice your Lamaze breathing," Sophie suggested. "They'll surely draw blood." She clicked the keychain to unlock her little Nissan.

Frowning at the cold as well as the information, Caroline hopped into Sophie's little brown car and fastened her seatbelt.

Forty minutes later, a nurse in scrubs retrieved the urine sample Caroline had left in the bathroom and ushered both ladies into a cotton-ball-white box of an examination room to meet with Dr. Strobel, Caroline's physician.

Sophie perched on the chair nearby.

Caroline rubbed the sore spot on her inner elbow. "As if morning sickness, sore breasts and fatigue aren't enough, now the vampires have to get in on it."

Sophie laughed. "Wimp. Wait until delivery. You'll be begging for the IV so they can put medicine in it."

"Not me," Caroline vowed. "No meds."

Sophie rolled her eyes. "That's what they all say. We'll see if you manage it when you can hardly get a blood draw without blubbering like a baby."

"I did not," Caroline pouted. *I love that we can banter and be playful. It breaks the tension a bit.*

A knock on the door interrupted their teasing. "Well, hello, Caroline," said the friendly-looking man of fifty. She noted with amusement that he'd let his hair grow a little too long. It curled around his collar. "What can I do for you today? Are you having some trouble?"

"No, doctor. I'm pregnant." Despite the tension at work and the oppressive morning sickness, she couldn't stop grinning.

"Ah, congratulations. I assume this is a good thing?" He raised both eyebrows.

"Yes. It's planned," she replied.

"Well very good then." He smiled. "About how far along are you?"

She considered. "I'm not sure. I've read a bunch of stuff, and I really don't understand how to measure the weeks."

"That's not surprising. We actually start counting on the first day of your last menstrual period, which is usually about two weeks before conception takes place."

"So my pregnancy started before I got pregnant?"

"Yes." His eyes crinkled in the corners as he reacted to her succinct question.

"How odd. Okay, let me think. I had my period about five weeks ago."

"Okay." He noted the information on his chart. "How are you feeling?"

"Sick," she replied. Even now her belly once again began churning and threatened to expel its contents. "I knew about morning sickness, but I had no idea it would be this bad. None of the remedies work."

His eyebrows drew together. "Are you vomiting frequently?"

"Yes, about four or five times each day."

He looked even more taken aback. "That is a lot. Hmmm. I might be able to give you a prescription for that."

"I would greatly appreciate it," she replied. "I almost can't keep anything down."

The doctor regarded the chart, his face twisting into a serious expression. "You know, at only five weeks you shouldn't be feeling much morning sickness yet. Are you sure you're not further along?"

Caroline shook her head. "No, I didn't start trying until three weeks ago."

"But were you sexually active before?" he pressed.

Caroline thought about it. "How long before?"

"From the symptoms you're describing, I would say at least a month."

A month before I had sex with Victor in my office. Shit. This isn't good. She took a slow deep breath. "Yes, once in that time frame," she admitted, "but we used a condom."

He shook his head. "That's not a guarantee."

"And I had my period," she insisted.

"Bleeding can happen in pregnancy. It might not have been a period." The doctor regarded her with lowered eyebrows and a puzzled expression.

Caroline covered her face with her hands. *It's not possible. How could it be? After trying so hard to have a baby with Victor…? No. I won't even think it. There's no way.* "Is that the only possible explanation?"

"No," he admitted. "There are many possible reasons."

"How can I know for sure?" she pleaded. "It's really important."

"Why?" he asked.

She blinked. *Why would it not be?* she wondered, forgetting that he had no idea what she'd been up to for the last couple of months.

"I mean," he said, addressing her obvious bewilderment, "we do need to know so we can determine your due date, but really, why does it make such a difference to you?"

Caroline didn't reply. Tears burned the corners of her eyes.

Sophie answered for her. "Because two months ago it was the wrong daddy."

The doctor leveled on Caroline a darkly disapproving scowl.

She choked on a sob and began sniffling.

Sophie walked over and slung an arm around her shoulders.

Dr. Strobel schooled his face back neutrality. "Let's just get an ultrasound. That way we can see what's going on."

131

"Thank you," Caroline replied in a fervent, watery voice.

～

About half an hour later, Caroline hadn't stopped crying. Slow tears ran constantly down her cheeks. Despite Sophie urging her not to panic, she couldn't stop. *I thought I wanted a baby, any baby, but now I only want Victor's.* "What am I going to do?" she asked Sophie for the hundredth time, as they sat together on a low bench with a red vinyl cushion, waiting for the ultrasound technician to get the machine ready.

"You're going to calm down and let the doctor do his work," Sophie replied. "We don't know anything yet. Most likely it's nothing, a mistake. What else could it be?"

"I don't know. This has to be Victor's baby," she whimpered. "It just can't be William's."

Sophie shook her head. "Don't even think about it, honey. One time? With a condom? No, it's much more likely to be a mistake."

"Even so, it just kills me."

"What does, Caroline?"

She sobbed and somehow the sound released a flood of sorrow and guilt. "That I was with William at all. Victor wanted me years ago, you know, a whole semester before William and I even met. I was really attracted to him too. I wanted him so much, but I was determined to be good, and then I wasted three years of my life, two of them in bed with the wrong man."

"You couldn't be with Victor when he was in your class," Sophie reminded her gently.

"Of course not," Caroline wiped her eyes, even as fresh tears took the place of the ones she dashed away, "but how hard would it have been to tell him that he shouldn't take any more classes from me, that he should be my boyfriend instead? He would have been over-joyed, and there would have been no question about whose baby I was having. It's weird. I went to bed with Victor so easily, and I feel great about it, but I feel terrible about William, even though I made him wait so long. Why is that?" *Oh God, I'm babbling so bad. I'm so glad I have friends who will listen to me.*

"Because you love Victor," Sophie explained. "It was obvious from the moment I saw you together, and it feels right to sleep with someone you love. You never loved William, so no amount of time could have made that feel right."

"Why did I do it then?"

"So you wouldn't be alone." Sophie patted her arm.

"Alone with the love of my life just across campus. God, I'm stupid."

Sophie opened her mouth to reply but another voice from down the hall interrupted. "Caroline, we're ready for you."

Caroline stood unsteadily and staggered into the ultrasound room—another sterile white box, but this one crowded with a ridiculous amount of equipment. The technician, a young woman with short, spiky black hair, helped Caroline onto the table. Sophie took a seat off to the side. Caroline supposed that was where fathers normally sat.

"Okay, slip off your panties and put your feet in the stirrups," she said, draping a sheet over Caroline's midsection.

What? Try though she might, she could make nothing of the instruction. "Why?" she demanded.

"For your ultrasound," the tech replied, as though it should be obvious.

I have a bad feeling about this. "I thought that was done over my belly."

"It's too early for that. You need a transvaginal ultrasound. Here."

133

She handed Caroline a long wand wrapped in a plastic sheath, heavily lubricated.

Caroline looked at the girl. "Are you kidding me?" she asked, appalled.

"No. We get the best detail this way."

Caroline sighed and followed directions, wincing. *What a strange sensation. Thank God I wore a skirt today.*

The technician took the handle of the wand from Caroline's hand and began adjusting it, looking at a monitor as she worked.

Caroline bit her lip and tried not to squirm.

Just as the woman got the instrument into the position she wanted, Dr. Strobel strode in. "Are you ready, Judy?"

"Yes, sir," the tech replied.

"Okay, let's take a look."

The shadowy gray images on the screen meant nothing to Caroline, nor did the jargon the doctor and his tech threw back and forth to each other. Finally, she couldn't take it anymore. "What's happening?" she demanded.

"You were right," he told her, looking pleased again, though not as strongly as before.

Well, you don't approve of your behavior, so why should anyone else?

"You're about five weeks pregnant."

"Thank God." Caroline sagged with relief. *Victor's baby. Just as I wanted.* "Then why...?"

"With twins."

Caroline's jaw dropped. "Twins?"

"Yes. Fraternal twins. Look." He indicated a pulsing oval on one side of the screen. "Here's one embryo. And there's the other." He pointed to a similar shape a short distance away.

"Oh my God," Caroline breathed, sinking back onto the padded table.

"That's why you've been so sick," the doctor continued in his pedantic way. "It's not a huge surprise. As a woman ages, her body is more likely to release two eggs at a time. You're not that old, but every year counts." He patted her leg. "It's a blessing, Caroline. You've been actively trying to get pregnant. You've succeeded in a big way."

"I guess so. Wow! What does this mean?" All previous experiences with 'overwhelmed' paled in comparison to this moment. *Don't ask me my name, age or occupation right now. I'd probably answer in Pig Latin.*

"Yes, doctor," Sophie piped up, sounding worried, "Caroline is really small. Is she going to be okay?"

"Well, twins are a high-risk pregnancy, but not critically so," he reassured her. "You'll need some extra monitoring of course, and you will likely need a cesarean delivery, but you should be fine."

Caroline made an inarticulate sound and then fell silent.

"Well, that about wraps things up," Dr. Strobel announced. "Now that I know what's happening, I'm content to watch and see."

Judy pulled the probe out of Caroline's vagina.

She winced at the nasty, squishy sensation. *I need my underwear. I'm too damned exposed already.*

The doctor continued speaking. "I'll write you the prescription we talked about and the lab will process your bloodwork... oh, and I'll ask the nurse to get you some pamphlets on health in pregnancy and multiples."

Caroline nodded numbly.

Dr. Strobel strode out of the room without further comment, the technician trailing after her.

Caroline slowly pulled on her underwear. She felt like she was floating. Nothing seemed real.

"You'd better call Victor," Sophie said finally.

Caroline shook her head. "Not yet."

"Why?" Sophie demanded.

Yes, why? There's a reason why. Come on, thoughts.

Gel, would you? At last, the maelstrom stilled enough for Caroline to form coherent sentences. "He's in a final."

Sophie scrunched her face. "Isn't this more important than a test?"

Caroline shook her head again, both in disagreement and to clear her still-hazy mind. "No, listen. Twins, Sophie. I wasn't sure I wanted to keep working so much when I thought it was just one baby. Now there's no way. I'm going to have to cut back my work to almost nothing. It's vital that Victor finish his degree as well and as quickly as possible so he can get a good job and provide for us." *There's another reason. What was it? My head is still so fuzzy. That work thing. Ugh. Victor getting his degree finished is very important.*

"Is he willing to do that?" Sophie asked, wide-eyed.

"Yes. Not only willing but eager." A slow smile spread across Caroline's lips, though she had not fully regained control of herself.

"You know," Sophie told her, "I would have a hell of a time with that. Don't get me wrong, he seems great, but you've only been together three weeks. Are you sure you can trust him?"

"Yes, Sophie. We've been friends a lot longer than three weeks. I've known him for years. You do remember that, right?" Caroline reminded her friend.

"As a student," Sophie chided, narrowing her eyes. "He didn't tell you his life story when he was writing essays in your freshman English class."

Caroline sighed. *And here, at last, is the questioning I've been expecting.* "He told me more than you might think. I know his character. He's one of the most honest, responsible people I've ever met."

"I hope you're right, but aren't you worried?" Sophie prodded.

"Hell yes, I'm worried, but what choice do I have?" Caroline demanded. "I have to trust him. That means I have to let him finish his finals without distracting him. I'll tell him when he's done."

Cowed by Caroline's sudden aggression, Sophie backed down. "Oh, okay."

Crap, I overdid it. Settle down, Caroline, while you still have friends.

She opened her mouth to apologize when Dr. Strobel bustled back into the room. "Here you go," he said, handing Caroline a bundle of paper. "A prescription for anti-nausea medication as well as some pamphlets on pregnancies in general and multiple pregnancies in particular. I know it might be a challenge, but nutrition is going to be vital, so I've added a high-powered prenatal vitamin as well. Take it before bed so it doesn't upset your stomach. Call me if you have any questions or concerns, and we'll see you in a month."

Numbly, Caroline nodded and meandered out the door. In the waiting room, she stared at the seats, lost.

"Come on, hon," Sophie said, grabbing her arm and tugging her toward the door.

"Where are we going?" Caroline asked.

Sophie sighed. "Hormones times two. Caroline, snap out of it. I know you must feel like cotton-brain, but try to focus. We're going back to work, by way of the pharmacy."

Caroline nodded. "Right. Work." She shook off her hazy dreaminess. "I have papers to grade. That's going to be a challenge." Her stomach rumbled and churned.

"Let's pick you up some lunch while we're at it," Sophie suggested. "I might help perk you up."

"Agreed."

By the time they had finished running errands and returned to the University, Caroline's distraction had burned away somewhat, leaving her able once again to focus. As she munched contentedly on her fast-food salad, she pondered the situation. *For now, only my closest friends will know about the twins.* She touched her belly thoughtfully. *It isn't a bad thing, although I'm going to be very uncomfortable, especially in the summer.*

She finished her salad and washed down her new pills with a carton of milk before picking up a pile of exams. Deep in thought, a knock on the door startled her and she jumped. Looking up, she saw her friend and colleague, Dr. Burke. "Hi, Michael. What can I do for you?"

"I'm sorry if I startled you," the towering, black-haired professor apologized. "Dr. Miller asked me to come and talk to you. Are you all right?"

"Yes, I'm fine. Come in. Take a seat."

He stalked into the room and sank into one of her conference chairs.

Wow, he looks different, she thought. *He used to be such a mess... all scraggly hair and ill-fitting clothes. Being with Sheridan has really been the making of him. He looks like he actually believes in himself now.* With new, properly fitted clothing, his hair smoothed into a sleek ponytail, he had developed a smoldering sexiness she had never noticed before, and Sheridan was keeping it all for herself.

That's all right. At six feet six, he's far too tall to be interesting to me anyway. I prefer my dark and handsome men to be less than a foot taller than me, but it warms my heart to see Michael happy. "So what's up?" she asked.

"Well, first of all, I need Nick Randall's essay and his final exam. I've been asked to grade them."

Caroline grinned. *Michael's such a hard-ass about grading, Nick's gonna get an even worse score.* "Okay, sure." She fished out the paper and handed it to him.

"Do you have a rubric you give the students?"

"Yes. I'll get you one." *Should have guessed he'd need that,* she thought, rummaging in the low filing cabinet beside her desk. *I see I'm still a bit fuzzy.* She extracted another paper, which she gave to her colleague.

"Dr. Miller is also having me get copies of essays you've graded for other students," Michael explained.

"Who?" she asked.

"Well, your boyfriend for one," Michael explained. "Can you ask him to get me as many samples as he can, please?" At Caroline's nod, Michael continued. "Also other, random students of my choice. I've already spoken with three people I happen to know had us both." He patted the back of her hand. "As far as I'm concerned, the job is to be sure you're applying your grading rubric fairly to everyone."

"No problem." She paused a moment and then dared to ask, "Michael, is everyone furious with me about this?"

He shrugged, and his relaxed, neutral expression spoke volumes. "I'm not sure. For myself, I'm having a hard time seeing it as anyone else's business. I mean, students have the right to request their work regraded, but that doesn't mean you did anything wrong, and as for the rest, that's your private life and none of my concern."

Caroline heaved a sigh. "I wish everyone saw it that way."

Michael started to speak once, then twice, before finally blurting out, "Honestly, were you with... what's his name?"

"Victor."

"Were you with him then, when he was in your class?" His copper cheeks darkened.

"No. We got together three weeks ago," she insisted. "Before that, it was strictly a teacher-student relationship."

He nodded. "Okay. If you say so, I believe you. You've never been anything but professional as far as I've seen, and I'm certainly not in a position to throw any stones."

His support warmed her. *I think Michael may have just become more a true friend than a friendly colleague.* "Thank you." She smiled, though she knew it looked tense. The grin faded as the gravity of the situation burst back into her mind. "But please don't take sides. Be impartial. It's in everyone's best interest if you're above reproach. I always thought I was, but a reputation is a very fragile thing, isn't it?"

"It is." His lips twisted in a parody of a grin, an expression he used to make much more often. "Particularly when people have a vested interest in lying," he added, telling her subtly that he didn't feel impartial, and already knew what he expected to find.

He'll find what he's expecting all right, but hopefully, anyone looking will see the same thing, no matter their preconceived notions might be. "Right," she agreed. "Thanks for your help."

"You're welcome, Caroline, and good luck." He extended a hand, a little awkwardly.

Still working on that confidence thing, eh, big guy? Ah well. Glad to see he's improving. She laid her tiny palm against his huge one. "Thanks."

Michael rose to his feet and in two long-legged strides, reached the hallway and disappeared.

Caroline sighed with relief. *Michael Burke is a fair and honest man. He never takes it easy on anyone, but he will make sure the truth is brought to light. Come what may, I know the situation will be handled correctly.*

She graded a few more tests. *The kiddos did pretty well overall this semester,* she thought, feeling a tiny bit proud of herself. Another knock broke her concentration. This time, she saw the strawberry blond hair and scrawny figure of Alyssa Miller.

"Hi, how are you?" Caroline rose from the desk and greeted her former student warmly, placing a hand on her shoulder. Alyssa's bones forced the skin forward sharply and sucked in between. *That's all the more disturbing since she's wearing a sweater. I shouldn't be able to feel so much.*

"Hi, Dr. Jones." The young woman's face twisted

with worry, and she babbled, "Sorry to interrupt. I know you're busy grading, but I had to ask you something. Dr. Burke has asked me to turn in all the papers I wrote in your class that you graded. What does he need them for? Did I do anything wrong?"

Whoa. She sounds terrible. "No, Alyssa. It's not you," Caroline explained, wondering why such a simple request had produced such a strong reaction. "One of my students has questioned my grading policies and they need a baseline from students who aren't involved in the situation so that they can see whether I've been fair. Don't worry. It's got nothing to do with you. You're not in trouble."

"Oh, that's good." Alyssa sighed, hands trembling.

Caroline scanned the young woman's emaciated frame again and then stepped away around her desk. Her salad and milk had decided to do an uncomfortable tap dance in her belly, and her snack no longer appealed, so she opened her desk drawer. Pulling out a granola bar and an apple, she placed them into the student's hands. "Please go eat these right now. Don't give them to anyone else. You need to keep your strength up so you can finish your finals."

"I don't need this." And yet, Caroline saw a manic light in Alyssa's eyes as she stared at the food, as though she hadn't eaten in quite a while.

"Yes you do," Caroline insisted. "Please, Alyssa. It would make me feel much better."

Alyssa took a bite of the apple. She looked close to tears. "School is so hard," she said quietly.

"I know." Caroline laid a gentle hand on the girl's shoulder, trying not to shudder at its excessive boniness. "When do you finish?"

"I have three more semesters."

Three? Oh God, no. "You need to look into some kind of help. You won't make it at this rate."

"I can handle it," Alyssa insisted, a stubborn look on her face.

Caroline sighed. "Please let me know if there's anything I can do. Also… there's a student food bank in the administration building, you know, for that end of the month gap. Please, check it out."

Alyssa bit her lip, her pride that rejected the suggestion of charity warring with the thought of a meal she could afford.

To spare the young woman, Caroline returned to the point, adding, "In the meanwhile, do you still have those essays?"

Alyssa smiled, the macabre grin of a fleshless skull. "Yes. You always told us not to throw away graded work. I have them at my apartment."

"Good. Just give them to Dr. Burke, and I appreciate it very much."

Alyssa dipped her chin and turned to leave, trying hard to nibble the granola bar daintily, but her expression said she would rather wolf the whole thing down in two bites. Caroline had never looked starvation in the face before and found it deeply disturbing. *I'm so thankful I don't live in poverty.*

She returned to her exams and managed to complete the stack and calculate the semester grades: the usual complement of As and Bs, with a few Cs and a couple of kids who stopped showing up for class mid-semester and wouldn't pass.

She uploaded the grades that had been completed— all but Nick's—and began contemplating her next final: Victorian Period literature, a favorite of hers. *The seniors in that class are delightful, hardworking, clever young people. I'll miss them.* She glanced at the clock. *Goodness, Victor's exam is taking a long time. I hope there isn't a problem with it.*

Her hands went to her belly, and she smiled. *This is going to be very interesting.*

"Hi, Caroline."

She focused her dreamy gaze on the beautiful brown eyes of the man she loved. "Victor, what are you doing here?"

"I came to see you. I missed you." He moved to circle the desk.

"Please stay on that side," she urged, holding up her hand. "I've been talking to people about my 'unprofessional behavior' all week and I can't afford any questions."

"Sure." He plunked down in the seat across from her, but his frowning eyebrows told her his nonchalance had been entirely concocted.

"How did your test go?" she asked, trying to erase the disappointed look from his face.

He shrugged. "It was hard, but I think I did fine."

"That's good news. Do you have others today?"

"Only one. It won't be bad, though. Political Science. Just a scantron test, and I only need about thirty percent to get an A in the class."

"I've had that happen a time or two. How nice."

"It helps," he agreed. "How did the appointment go?"

"Fine. The doctor gave me medication for the nausea. Hopefully, I won't throw up quite so much. He did discover something interesting though."

"What's that?" Victor's eyebrows drew together, creating the typical little 11 between them.

And no wonder. When doctors find something interesting, it's usually bad. But not this time. "Well, he said we were more successful than we expected."

One eyebrow shot up, crinkling his forehead with questions. "Uh, what does that mean?"

"It's twins, Victor."

Victor made a sound, a sort of inarticulate wheeze, after which he sat blinking for the longest time.

"Yeah. A lot to take in, isn't it?" she commented.

"It is." He gulped. "Are you… happy?"

"Yes. I guess I am. Startled, nervous, but happy. I've always wanted a big family. I had hoped, even at my age, to be able to have at least two children. Now I do." A slow smile spread across her face. She brushed her fingertips over her belly.

He reached across the desk. "Do I really have to be good?" he wheedled, dark eyes pleading. "I'd like to hug you right now."

And I want that hug so much, but… She placed her free hand in his. "Better not. We can hug tonight."

His face fell. "Okay."

What a sweetheart. I wonder why I ever doubted my love for him. "Listen, Victor, I have to go give another final in a few minutes, but I'll see you tonight, okay?"

"Okay, Caroline. Take it easy."

"I will." She scanned the hallway, and, seeing no one, blew Victor a kiss.

The gesture made him smile. He squeezed her hand gently, and they walked in opposite directions.

~

Once Caroline disappeared out of sight, Victor sank heavily into a blue plastic chair, one of a row that stretched along the side of the hallway, attached to the floor with a chrome frame.

Twins. Lord, now what am I going to do? One thing's for sure. Having waited so long to have children, Caroline is not going to want to put our twins in daycare all day, every day. She'll be lucky to finish the spring semester, and after that, it will get a lot harder for her to keep up with everything. It's soon going to be up to me to handle my share of the finances, which is fine. I want to contribute anyway.

Pulling out his cell phone, he dialed the number of the engineering firm he had interned with the last three summers.

144

"Thorndyke Associates," a familiar female voice said.

"Hi, Angie, it's Victor Martinez. Can I please talk to Mr. Anderson?"

"Sure, Victor." After a beep and a few moments of canned hold music, the call transferred to the office manager.

"Anderson."

Victor took a deep breath. *Be bold, Martinez. Your family needs you.* "Mr. Anderson, this is Victor Martinez. How are you doing?"

"Pretty well, what I can I do for you, Victor?"

He sounds relaxed and… glad to hear from me. That's good. Victor bit one fingernail while he pondered his words. "Well, I'm just wondering something. Last summer you mentioned that I should call you when I graduate and you would see if there is a position available. I'm graduating in May, and I'd like to know, do you anticipate any openings at that time?"

"In May?" in the pause, Victor could hear a mouse clicking. "Not really, but we do have an associate retiring later in the summer. He's been here a long time. Most likely what will happen is that everyone under him will be promoted, freeing up an entry-level position. Would that interest you?"

"Would it ever! That would be perfect." *Thank you, all the powers that be!*

"Great. Stop by soon and fill out the paperwork so we're ready. There are no guarantees of course, but everyone here already knows you, so you have a better than usual shot."

Victor exhaled in a noisy whoosh that crackled through the phone. "Oh, thank God."

"You sound a little stressed," Mr. Anderson pointed out. "Is anything wrong?"

Victor considered how to explain the situation to the conservative office manager. "Not wrong, no, but my, um, my fiancée and I are expecting, and I wanted to be sure I could, you know, provide for them."

"Ah, well that's good then," the man replied, sounding unoffended. "I think it's likely we can help you. I know a lot of people would be really glad to have you here. I'll put in a good word for you myself."

"Thanks, Mr. Anderson."

"You're welcome. Have a good day, Victor, and come in soon, okay?"

"Of course. Goodbye."

He hung up. *Working at Thorndyke's would be great. I always liked it there. I'll stop by next week.*

CHAPTER 8

*C*couple of days later, Michael Burke stopped by Dr. Miller's office with a sheaf of graded papers in his hands. "Afternoon, Howard," he said, laying the pile on the department chair's desk.

"Michael, how's it going?"

They shook hands and Michael dropped carelessly into one of the hard, wooden seats. "I'm fine. Have any plans for the holiday?"

"Spending Christmas with my wife's family in Phoenix this year. What about you?"

"I'm going to meet Sheridan's parents," Michael informed him.

"Good luck." Dr. Miller waggled his bushy white eyebrows and smirked.

"Thanks." Michael colored, hating to discuss personal items with his stuffy colleague.

Dr. Miller seemed to decide he'd had enough interpersonal interaction. He returned to the topic at hand, his face sinking into its usual disapproving scowl. "So, what did you find out?"

Relieved to be back to business, Michael waved his hand over the sheaf of papers on the desk. "I graded Mr. Ramsey's research paper. I can't imagine she found anything to work with there. It was terrible. I wouldn't have even tried to find enough points for a D. I used her scoring rubric, and to be honest, I only found about 52 points. His final exam looked to be a C."

"And she graded the essay?"

"60."

Howard nodded slowly. "What other students did you look at?"

"I chose three who have previously taken my class, so I have some idea what to expect from them: Alyssa Miller, Hallie Gonzalez, and Marcus Guo. Using the scoring rubric she gave me, I regraded all of their essays myself. She applied her rubric pretty consistently. Honestly, I would have given all those essays grades pretty similar to what she did."

"And Victor's?"

"I have several of his essays and papers here." Michael reached into his briefcase and pulled out another stack of papers, waving them at his supervisor. "You know, people say I'm a tough professor, but she leaves me in the dust. She was so hard on that guy. He's getting Bs all over the place on papers I would not have hesitated to give an A, and you know I don't give many As."

"So she didn't elevate his grade?" Howard demanded.

"I don't see any evidence of it," Michael replied, making no attempt to disguise his trademark intensity.

The department chair eyed him for a long moment, as though weighing the information against his own internal measuring stick.

Come on, man. Even if you're not comfortable with her relationship, it doesn't automatically follow that she did anything unethical.

Dr. Miller returned his attention to the papers, thumbing through them and then closing them with a shuffle, his hand thumping on the desk. "All right then.

We can in good conscience tell Mr. Ramsey that his D is a gift and he should be quiet about it?"

"I would be completely comfortable with that," Michael assured him.

Dr. Miller sighed, his pale cheeks pinkening. "So that just leaves the situation with Caroline. Michael, what's your opinion about this?"

Michael resisted the urge to roll his eyes. "I don't have one. It's not my business. Caroline is a professional. She was fair and consistent in her grading. The rest has nothing to do with me."

"But don't you think it's a little embarrassing for the department?" Howard asked, a hint of a whine in his voice.

"How?"

"Victor Martinez is a student. He used to be her student."

Heat flared in Michael's face, but he remained calm and resolute on the surface. *Howard needs to separate his personal squeamishness from his job, or he won't remain department chair much longer.* "So what? Sheridan used to be my student. That's not going to stop me from proposing to her over the holiday."

"She's not a student at all anymore," Dr. Miller pointed out.

"And after next semester Victor won't be either."

"But Caroline's pregnant."

Michael's hint of heat turned to a painful flame. "No, I refuse to comment. It's irrelevant." *Also none of my business. Come on, man. Leave it be. This is not something we should be discussing. It's an HR situation.* He shifted in his seat, distinctly uncomfortable.

Dr. Miller gave Michael a quizzical look. Then he shook his head and released an inarticulate rumbling sound. "I really don't want to lose my two best female instructors at once."

Enough. Who knew full professor would come with so

much baggage? "Then don't. I believe Sheridan is looking to work part-time, you know, after. I'll let her talk to you about it though. I have no idea what Caroline's plans are. She might want to keep working."

"She's up for tenure in the spring."

"Oh. Well, that's good," Michael replied. *It's such a relief when tenure is approved, and in her situation, she needs all the good news she can get.*

"I don't know if I can recommend her after this mess."

Michael's jaw clenched. *You must be joking. Come on, seriously? This is unethical, bordering on illegal. If he carries out this threat, she'd have real cause for a discrimination suit.* He closed his eyes and shook his head. *They appointed me to a role that involves supplemental leadership for the department. That means it's my job to give the chair insight. My friend needs my help and fully deserves it.* Michael laid the situation out bluntly. "This mess is a lazy jock trying to get a grade he doesn't deserve. It's not Caroline's fault. It could have happened to anyone. Imagine the disaster if someone accused me."

The department chair sighed deeply. "Yes, but everyone's worked with Sheridan. We all know what a good student she was."

"Well," Michael replied, struggling for the calm, reasonable tone that would ensure Dr. Miller's continued attention and avoid a tantrum. "Victor's not an English major, but you could call the engineering department and talk to those professors, find out more that way."

The white-crested head bobbed. His stern expression relaxed until Dr. Miller resembled a bloodhound. "Yes."

Steeling himself, Michael continued, putting himself firmly in Caroline's camp. *She asked for impartiality, but I can't do it. Not when the situation is so unfair.* "You know, I was talking to Alyssa Miller a little. She and Victor were in Caroline's class together. She told me that while it was clear he was infatuated with Caroline, she never acted less than professionally towards him. Alyssa even went to Caroline's office to ask a question, and he was there. The two of them were alone with the door open, sitting across the desk from each other, completely hands-off, talking about literary analysis. I think they're telling the truth that they just got together."

"I'm sure you'd like to believe that, since you're trying to promote the same story for yourself," Dr. Miller drawled sarcastically.

So that's how we're going to roll, is it? Caroline's not the only one who has evaluations coming up. Maybe it's time for fresh leadership in this department. "It's true, that's all," Michael said frankly, too frustrated to remain embarrassed. "In fact, I wish I had behaved less professionally. The years I wasted *not* being with Sheridan bother me a lot."

Dr. Miller stuck his neck out, which changed his image from hound dog to turkey. Then he shook away images that must have offended his high-strung sensibilities in a shudder that set his hair and jowls twitching. "Okay, don't tell me any more about that. Have a good Christmas. Congratulations on... everything. See you in January. Thanks for your help."

"You're welcome." Michael stood to leave, stiffly and with growing antipathy. *Get me out of here. This kind of nosy intrusiveness and closet sexism makes my skin crawl. How is it appropriate to be discussing a professional's private business behind her back?* The more Michael thought of it, the worse he felt. *At least I think she's off the hook for the grading fiasco.*

~

After Michael left, Dr. Miller began leafing through the pile of papers. *As Michael said, Caroline's grading appeared consistent, and she was particularly hard on Victor.*

A quick glance at Nick's essay revealed that it really

was no better than she had said, and maybe a little worse. Frowning, Dr. Miller called the kinesiology department chair and explained the situation.

Upon hearing that his freshman tackle had turned in a research paper without a works cited page, despite clear verbal and written warnings from the professor, the coach completely agreed with the decision to put Nick on academic probation and pull him from active athletics participation. Football season had just ended, but he was involved in several other sports. Nicholas Ramsey would be spending at least one semester warming a lot of benches in disgrace. If he turned it around, he might be able to play in the fall, but that would be up to him.

Much relieved, Dr. Miller placed one more phone call, to the chair of the engineering department. "Dr. Williamson?" he said into the receiver.

"Yes, can I help you?" a nasal voice replied.

"This is Dr. Miller, the English department chair."

"What's up?" the voice asked. He cleared his throat.

"We've had a little situation come up over here with one of your students—" Dr. Miller began, but Dr. Williamson cut him off.

"Oh? Who's that?"

"Victor Martinez."

A resounding snort caused the phone connection to crackle. "Victor's involved in a situation? I find that hard to believe."

"Believe it. He appears to have moved in with his former English professor and gotten her pregnant." Dr. Miller held the phone away from his ear to muffle the sound of loud guffaws.

Dr. Williamson forced out his words between gasping wheezes. "I wouldn't have believed he had it in him." He sounded impressed, as well as amused.

"Why is that?" Dr. Miller demanded.

"Because he's so shy." Dr. Williamson took an audible breath and when he had calmed, he continued. "Okay, so she's not his professor anymore?"

"No, not in over a year," Dr. Miller admitted, "but that's not really the issue. A student has taken exception to it, saying she's not grading fairly. Victor did really well in her classes, so I'm trying to find out if he does well overall."

"He does," Dr. Williamson replied without hesitation. "He's a straight-A student. He's really bright, and like a lot of our non-trads, he knows how to work hard."

"He's non-traditional?" As he voiced the question, Dr. Miller recalled Caroline mentioning something of the sort.

"Yes, he's over thirty. From what he's said, he was in the Army and then worked in a retail store for a while first. Uh, how old is she?"

"Early thirties." *Maybe it does kind of make sense, but still. How awkward.*

"Ah, well I can see it then. You don't need to worry about Victor. If he got a good grade in her classes, it wasn't because she was doing anything wrong. Victor's the kind of man who asks to be graded harder because he wants to get as close to perfection as possible. If he got an A, he earned it many times over."

"That's good to know."

The two professors hung up, Dr. Williamson still chuckling a little at the thought of timid Victor Martinez scoring with a professor. "That boy has cojones after all."

There was only one thing left to do. Dr. Miller called Caroline into his office and offered her a seat.

She sank gratefully into the uncomfortable chair. "Yes, sir?" Her face had turned an interesting shade of green and he noticed her hands, which were clasped in front of her, trembled.

"Are you all right?" he asked, concerned. *I hope she doesn't vomit on my desk.*

She swallowed. "Yes. What did you need me for?"

"Michael has done a very thorough job going over your grading. Everything appears to be in order. You're off the hook for Nick. I'm still not comfortable with this situation you've put yourself in, but you haven't violated the University's policy, so that's the end of that. The incident will be recorded in your file as a student who asked his work to be regraded, which was done, and your original grade upheld."

"Thank you, sir." Now Caroline looked close to tears.

"I do need to know one thing though. Okay, you're expecting." *This line of questioning is so uncomfortable. I hate it. Working with young women isn't my favorite. Things like this are always coming up.*

"Yes," she stated plainly.

"When is the baby due?"

"July."

"So you won't need maternity leave in the spring?"

She shook her head slowly, as though the movement felt uncomfortable. "I don't think so unless something goes wrong."

"That's good. What about the fall?"

Caroline made a face. "I don't know yet. Dr. Miller, I've waited a long time to become a mother. My inclination is to limit myself to four classes only, no overloads, but I don't want to jeopardize my position." She sighed. "Next year will not be my year for career-building, but I don't want to quit altogether."

He nodded. *I expected as much.*

"But I don't know if I will be able to. It will depend on a lot of things, so I'll have to play it by ear, I suppose."

"When will you know?" he asked.

"I'm not sure. Will I... still have a job here in the fall?" She bit her lip, worry creasing her features.

"I think it's likely," he admitted reluctantly. "As you said before, you've done an excellent job preparing yourself for tenure. The other professors and most of the students like you, and your work speaks for itself. I'm sure you'll get the department recommendation. After that, it has to go through the channels, but it's rare for tenure to be rejected if the department recommends it."

She closed her eyes. "Thank you." Her voice wavered.

She sounds miserable. Maybe I should back off a bit. "Are you coming to the Christmas party tonight?"

Caroline cocked her head to one side at the abrupt change of topic. "I'll see how I'm feeling."

"Right. Um, listen, I know spouses and significant others are usually invited, but please, spare my sensibilities. Don't bring him," Dr. Miller begged. "Not this year. If you're still together after he graduates, I'll try to make peace with it."

"Okay." Caroline swallowed, and then swallowed again, her throat contracting. "Sir, I don't mean to cut you off, but I'm not feeling well."

Yikes, she is going to throw up. "Oh, sorry. Go."

She ran out of the room.

CAROLINE'S CHOICE

CHAPTER 9

*T*hat night, Caroline skipped the Christmas party and stayed home, not to make a statement, but because she was exhausted. The medication had helped somewhat—instead of throwing up several times per day, she now managed about once every other day—but between the mess at work, uncertainty over her professional future, and trying to grow two babies at once, her stamina had collapsed. She ate a quick dinner of chicken and broccoli and went right to bed.

Victor slid in beside her and took her in his arms.

"Are you going to sleep now?" she asked drowsily, noticing the clock read 8:30.

"Probably not, but you look so pretty I want to hold you. Are you okay?" His warm brown eyes filled with concern.

"Yes. I'm just really tired," she admitted. "This last week has been too much for me."

"It'll be okay." He petted her back soothingly. "You're not going to have to deal with everything on your own anymore. We're a team now."

She smiled weakly. "I'm so glad that the semester is over. I'm going to need every day of this break to recover." Releasing a lungful of air, she let her tension melt away as she rested her forehead against his shoulder.

"Yes. You just take all the time you need, sweet girl. Relax. Rest." He kissed her.

"Victor?" Caroline said, voicing a thought that had been troubling her.

"Yes, love?"

"Um, I forgot to tell you. Every Christmas Eve, my mother has us all over. Would you be willing to go? I want you to meet my sisters." She winced as she voiced the invitation.

"Okay. We need to do that, don't we?" He sounded more relaxed than he had about meeting her friends.

His confidence is growing. Hope this doesn't set him back. She lifted her head. "Yes. I have to tell you, it's not going to be fun." She distracted herself from what was sure to be an unpleasant conversation by running her thumb over Victor's bottom lip.

"Why not?"

Don't pull your eyebrows together, honey. She touched the tiny 11 formed by his frown. "Well, you know how your mother comes on kind of strong, and a person has to get used to her?"

"Yes," Victor said cautiously.

"Don't take it wrong, baby. I love your mother. She's really warm and nice. Anyway, my mother comes on pretty strong too. Unfortunately, she's neither warm nor nice. Most likely she'll disapprove of you."

"Why?"

Caroline sighed. "She disapproves of everyone. In my whole life, I've only seen her like one person."

"And that was?"

"William."

Victor groaned. "Oh hell. Well, I don't have a chance then, do I?"

"No," Caroline admitted. "I'm sorry. It's not only that either. She's certainly going to take exception to your... heritage as well."

He sighed. "Caroline, why do I have to meet this woman?"

"I'm not taking you to meet her. I'm taking you to meet my sisters. Mom's just part of the package. You know I don't share her... bias. I love your Mexican side. I love you. Can't you please go, meet my sisters, and try to ignore her? Everyone else does."

"I'll try, but to be honest, that kind of prejudice really bothers me." His face turned harsh.

She pressed a tender kiss to his lips, which softened his expression tremendously. "I know. She's a mean-spirited bigot. That's her problem, not yours."

"Do you have a dad, Caroline?" he asked.

She nodded, smiling despite her fatigue. "Yes. He left her the day after my youngest sister graduated from high school. Said he wasn't going to waste another minute of his life saddled to an iceberg. He remarried a nice young woman a few years later and they have two little kids together. Very nice but very young. It's weird to see them together; him a grandpa of five... soon to be seven," she patted her belly, "and her not much older than me."

"Don't you visit him?" Victor asked, drawing her back to reality.

Caroline felt a stab of guilt. "I haven't in a while. You know looking at other people's babies drives me crazy. We talk on the phone."

"Well, let's visit him soon, okay? He sounds okay, and you don't have to be bothered by other people's kids anymore." He laid his hand on her tummy.

"You're right." She brightened for a moment before fatigue dragged another ferocious yawn out of her. "That's great. I've missed Dad a lot." She nestled down into the pillows, her eyelids closing of their own accord.

"Go to sleep, little teacher," Victor murmured. "I'll be good and go meet your mother and try not to take offense at her." He kissed her again, then once more.

Half drowsing, Caroline murmured, "I love you. I wish we could just get married." Then sleep dragged her under completely.

~

Victor lingered beside his beloved, arms around her, staring down into her peaceful face.

I'm amazed how much has changed over the last month. Hard to imagine that at Halloween I simply knew I would love this woman without reciprocation until life separated us for good. Then, in a moment, it all turned around. Amazing.

He traced her eyebrows with the tip of one finger. *So she wants to get married, does she? That's no surprise, after her previous boyfriend played with her for three years, not moving ahead but also not telling her had no such intentions.*

Well, I want to marry her. I really do, but how? I have no money for an engagement ring, let alone a whole wedding, and I don't want to do it on credit, not with twins on the way. So how can I give my precious Caroline what she wants?

An idea dawned on him and he slipped out of the bed and crept down to the den to call his mother.

CHAPTER 10

CHAPTER 10

*T*he next morning, despite going to bed so early, Caroline woke rather late. Perhaps too late, as her stomach felt uncertain in its emptiness. She feared getting out of the bed because of the nausea that was certain to result.

"Victor?" she called.

A moment later he poked his head in the door. "Yes?"

"Can you please bring me something to eat?" she begged, holding her belly.

His eyebrows drew together. "What would you like?"

"Anything. I just don't want to get up with an empty stomach." Already her guts had begun to churn.

"Okay, I'll see what I can find. Rest easy. I'll be right back."

He returned quickly with a banana, a glass of milk, and her pill. *Perfect. Not too sweet, not too starchy.* She ate the banana gratefully, washed down the pill with the milk and then waited several minutes before trying to move. Rising cautiously, Caroline took stock of her body. It seemed she had staved off nausea... this time.

She meandered along the hallway and down the stairs in search of coffee. By the time she reached the kitchen, Caroline had gone from nauseous to ravenous. *How strange. Well, the pamphlet on twin pregnancies did warn that frequent changes between sickness and hunger could be common. Looks like they were correct.*

She rummaged in the cabinets for her cookbook and began mixing up a batch of batter for waffles. *That sounds good. With butter and honey.*

"What are you up to?" Victor asked, approaching with a cup of coffee. "Is your belly ready for some coffee?"

She grabbed the cup and sipped it. "Ah. Now I'm starting to feel a little more human. Thank you. And to answer your question with a question, do you like homemade waffles?"

"I've never had any," he admitted, a frown creasing his lips. "Only the frozen kind. I have to confess, I'm not a big fan."

"Try mine before you decide," she boasted playfully. "The frozen ones are pretty disgusting."

One corner of his mouth flipped up and his eyes twinkled. "I'm game. Can I do anything?"

"Can you cook?" Caroline raised one eyebrow. *He hasn't made anything more complicated than sandwiches so far.*

"Yes…" he proclaimed proudly, and then snorted at himself and admitted, "Well, no. But I can grill, I'm good at putting canned things in the microwave, and I'm an expert cereal pourer."

She laughed. *He's so silly. Guess he's in a playful mood this morning.* "Good to know."

"Oh, but I do know how to mix a pretty good drink," he added.

Feeling playful herself, Caroline pouted. "And I'll not be trying your drinks for a year… probably more since I want to breastfeed."

"Hmmm. I hope you'll let me watch." He waggled his eyebrows at her and groped one breast.

Caroline laughed so hard she slopped waffle batter on the counter. "Naturally. They're your babies too. Of course you can watch." She suppressed the urge to purr as her sensitive breast reacted to his touch. *That feels so good. Later, after breakfast…*

"You know, not all mixed drinks have alcohol," he pointed out. "How about if I mix up something exotic that's perfectly healthy for you and the babies?"

"Sure." She kissed his cheek. "Give it a try."

The couple got to work on their separate tasks. As Caroline flipped a lovely golden brown waffle out of the steaming waffle iron, Victor touched a straw to her lips. "Tell me what you think of this."

"What is it?" she asked, pulling back and eyeing the purplish liquid suspiciously. *I see floaties in there.* The thought elicited a gag.

"Virgin sangria," he proclaimed proudly. "Didn't you say a while back that sangria was one of your favorites?"

Still swallowing down her revulsion, Caroline blurted, "Victor, sangria is nothing but wine, fruit, sugar and brandy. How can a virgin variety exist?"

"Well, there isn't really such a thing," he admitted. "This is actually grape juice with a dash of lemon juice to cut the sweetness and a few orange pieces. But it tastes good, and it gives you a couple of servings of fruit. Give it a try."

Okay, orange pieces. Nothing to worry about, right, stomach? Nothing scary in a couple of orange bits. She sipped and found it tasted good. She took another sip and then removed the cup from his hand, setting it on the counter so she could give him a long, wet kiss. Then she released him and poured more batter.

In another few minutes, she had two plates on the table with honey and butter, and Victor contributed a pitcher of his tasty juice concoction. He took a cautious bite of the waffle and Caroline beamed to see his eyes roll back in his head.

"That's amazing," he said, leaning over to kiss her cheek.

She blushed and sipped her drink. "So is this. What a great team we make."

A broad smile creased his face. "We do." He tucked in another bite, chewed and swallowed. "You know what I'm looking forward to?"

"What's that?" she finished her drink and poured another, careful to leave the orange bits in the pitcher.

"Doing nothing," he replied. "We've been so busy since Thanksgiving, that even though we live together —which is absolutely great by the way—we've hardly spent any time alone. I'm looking forward to relaxing with my sweet lady."

She sighed as happiness washed over her. "That does sound really nice. I hope you don't mean doing absolutely nothing though. I'm tired but not too tired to want to make out with my sexy boyfriend." She trailed her fingers over the arm of his sweater.

His teeth flashed and despite the thickness of the fabric, he seemed to shiver at the tickling touch. A quick glance revealed the front of his pants had grown rather full. "That sounds nice too. Oh, are you sure it's okay?"

"Yes, the doctor said sex during pregnancy is safe." Caroline smirked. *Thank goodness. I'm addicted now. If I couldn't get busy with my man, I think I might waste away.*

"Even with twins?" he pressed.

"Yes, unless something happens. Believe me, baby, I checked."

"Good girl. You think of everything, don't you?" He tugged gently on a lock of her hair, causing agreeable shivers to run down her spine, and then rested his fingertips on the table, drumming in a soothing rhythm.

"No, of course I don't, but I think about how much I love being with you." She covered his hand with hers.

"Would you like to do something fun today?" His expression turned cautiously hopeful, and she could see that whatever it was meant a great deal to him.

"Sure. What do you have in mind?"

"I'd love to get over to the museum. They have an exhibit about new technology that looks really interesting. Are you game? We can see the arts and antiquities too."

"Uh," she made a face. *Why that? Anything but that?* "I don't really like the museum," she admitted. "How set are you on going?"

His smile faded. "Wow, I've never heard of a professor who didn't like museums. It really doesn't fit with what I know about you. You're such an artsy type. Why don't you like it?"

She looked away.

"What?" Victor pressed.

"William works there," she blurted. *I don't want to see that... grrr, I can't even find the right word to describe him. Never again.*

He winced. "Really?"

"Yes," she admitted. "He's the assistant director."

Victor raised his eyebrows. "Wow, that's a prestigious position."

"Yes." *Bet that's why Mom likes him.*

"Okay, we don't have to go," Victor agreed easily, though his eyes remained sad.

Caroline pondered her options. *It's rare for Victor to ask for anything, and I really want to make him happy. How bad could it be? The odds of seeing William are pretty small. Okay, I can do this.* She took a deep breath. "No, let's go. I mean, he's not usually out wandering the exhibits. He has an office. There's no reason to suspect we would see him, and even if we did, so what? It's over. I'm with you now and this is exactly where I want to be. I love you, Victor. Let's go to the museum."

"Are you sure?"

"Yes. You can explain to me what we're looking at."

He beamed at her, and she knew she had made the right decision.

~

So they went, holding hands like any other couple. As they walked down hallways tiled in white with gold speckles, pausing to read the plaques and captions adorning the walls, he gave her a preview based on a newspaper article he'd read.

Then they entered the temporary exhibits room, a two-story space with round walls and a domed ceiling made entirely of skylights. Long pendant lamps suspended from below the second story balconies augmented the weak December sunlight. Hands-on experiments stationed in the cavernous space demonstrated alternate energy sources, renewable fuels, and the latest in windmills that were supposed to be bird-safe.

Caroline listened carefully as Victor enlightened her about everything they were seeing.

She was concerned before, but now it looks like she's having fun if that hint of a smile lingering around her lips means anything.

After a couple of hours, they finished exploring the science room and made their way to the antiquities exhibit. Caroline pulled Victor behind a huge statue of Apollo in a chariot and treated him to a thorough kiss. And then another, and another.

This is getting out of hand, he realized, trying—without much conviction—to disentangle himself from his beloved's embrace.

Caroline must have noticed his weak struggles. "Let's go home, baby," she whispered. "I'm ready to start doing nothing by spending the afternoon in bed. Would you like to join me there?"

His sex hardened to instant, aching fullness. "That sounds great. Let's go."

They slipped out from behind the statue and moved in the direction of the door, grinning like naughty teenagers, eager to be alone again.

"Carrie? Hey, Carrie?"

Caroline stopped dead. Her eyes closed. A tall and handsome man with a distinguished air and silver wings in his dark hair approached them, a blond woman hanging on his arm. She wore the tightest of skinny jeans on her round little bottom and a low-cut blouse.

"Jessica, William." Caroline's voice had turned carefully neutral, but her frown and the embarrassed squint in the corners of her eyes spoke volumes.

William's elegant appearance struck Victor. He finally understood what Caroline had seen in this man. On the surface at least, he looked like a woman's dream; attractive, dignified, and successful. And yet she had been willing to throw him over, to dump him, and take on Victor instead. *I won her when she had this man in her life and in her bed. Wow.*

"Hello, Carrie," the man said warmly.

Victor could hear Caroline's teeth grinding. "I've asked you many times not to call me that, William. Caries are cavities."

He snorted, waving a hand as though to dismiss her request. "That's ridiculous."

His insouciance irritated Victor, who dared to say, "It's her name. Let her go by what she chooses."

William glanced his way and raised one eyebrow, looking Victor up and down with a condescending air. "And who would this be?"

"This is Victor, my boyfriend." Caroline lifted her chin. "Victor, this is William LaGrange, the assistant director of this museum, and his… friend Jessica Barton."

Victor studied the couple but didn't speak. His

thoughts moved too fast for his mouth to form coherent words. *This is the one who brought Caroline to the party where she was assaulted. This is the man who treated her like a kinky sex doll and played with her heart the whole time. These two conspired to break Caroline's heart and undermine her confidence. What a couple of jerks. I'm glad they're out of her life.*

"Is this the new lover you told me about?" William asked, shaking Victor back to reality.

Victor gave Caroline a speaking look. "You told him about us?"

Caroline's frown turned violent. "I didn't tell him anything except that I was seeing someone. And I haven't talked to him since before Thanksgiving." She turned to William and his companion. "Well, I would say that it was good to see you, but I don't like to lie, so I guess I'll just go. Victor?"

"What's the rush?" Jessica wheedled. "I've missed you. I didn't want to stop being your friend."

Caroline nailed her with a harsh glare. "I don't need friends like you."

"How mean," she whined.

Caroline didn't respond.

Victor noticed William giving Caroline a hot, speculative look. *How strange, given she told me his interest in her began waning a year before they broke up.*

She turned towards her former lover and her eyes narrowed. "Stop it," she hissed in a poisonous, breathy snarl.

"No. I can look all I want." There was amusement in his tone that Victor didn't understand.

"You're disgusting." Caroline's face twisted into a pained expression. She looked ready to hurl... or cry.

William smirked at her, unperturbed by the insult. "You didn't used to think so."

"I didn't know what good love was. *You* certainly never showed me."

167

William quirked an eyebrow and drawled, "And he does? Is he really that good? Hmmm. I can see it now. It's just what you always longed for, isn't it? A sweet little vanilla boy to please you."

"Shut up." She turned and stalked away.

"You'll never forget, Carrie," he called after her.

"I've already forgotten," she shot back as she exited the building.

Victor hurried after her. He found her leaning against the car, staring at the slender cedar trees that lined the parking lot. Even from a distance, he could see her clenched jaw and fists.

"What was that all about?" he asked her mildly.

"Can you please hold me?" she begged, her lip trembling.

She looks so vulnerable. Poor Caroline. Victor wrapped his arms around her, trying to send her wordless encouragement *He's gone from your life, honey. We're making a new family now. The family you always wanted. Forget the past. He's nothing but a misstep.*

At last, she calmed in his arms, shoulders sagging.

Victor dared ask a risky question. "What was he doing that made you so angry?"

"Imagining us in bed." She shuddered. "I used to hate it when he did that to other couples. I never thought I would be on the receiving end."

Victor didn't let on how much that bothered him. For Caroline's sake, he pretended lightness. "Well, let him dream. Remember, little teacher, he never loved you like I do."

"Right."

Victor snorted.

"What?"

"I've never been called vanilla before. Aren't I a little dark for it?" He knew what William meant, but he made the dumb joke trying to distract Caroline.

She didn't take the bait. "He didn't mean your eth-

nicity, Victor. That was a comment on your sexual pro-
clivities. It's not a compliment. It kind of implied you're
boring in bed."

Victor gave up trying to be funny. "I'm glad *you*
don't agree. His opinion isn't very important."

"I know." She turned sad eyes up to him. "Victor,
doesn't it bother you that I used to be with him?"

Ah, so that's what has her so upset. He replied with
equally painful honesty. "Well, for your sake, yes. But I
can't be too upset about it. Don't forget, I have an embarrassing former partner too."

Her mouth curled into a humorless smile. "Oh, I did
forget that."

"There's one good thing though," Victor added,
trying again for levity.

"What's that?"

"You'll never miss him."

At last, Caroline gave a genuine smile. "No. How
can I?" She twined her arms around his neck.

"Well, that was awkward and unpleasant. Shall we
expand our afternoon plans to include a shower? I feel a
little contaminated."

"Can I go with you?" She gazed up at him with
puppy dog eyes.

He laughed. "I think that can be arranged."

Actually, the afternoon Victor and Caroline spent in
bed closely resembled what William had imagined. He
had pictured Caroline's pretty little body sprawled
naked on black satin sheets, twisting with pleasure
while Victor knelt between her legs, holding her thighs
in his hands as he treated her to deep, thorough thrusts,
really giving it to her good. He got everything right except the sheets. It was too cold for satin so they lay on
cream-colored flannel for the gentle lovemaking they
both enjoyed so much.

CHAPTER 11

Christmas Eve arrived, and Caroline drove Victor to her mother's home in the suburbs.

The exterior of the white two-story glittered with white lights that lined the eaves with ruler straightness and perfectly placed nets of the same stark color on the two evergreen bushes flanking the front door. *Leave it to Mom to make even Christmas lights look sterile and unwelcoming.*

Caroline clung to Victor's hand as they approached the black front door and knocked.

An attractive, middle-aged woman with carefully highlighted blond hair and a sour expression met them. "Caroline."

"Mother. Merry Christmas."

Cheryl didn't return the greeting. "Is this him then?" she asked, eyeing Victor, and her voice held no inflection whatsoever.

"Yes," Caroline agreed, trying to sound normal even as the tension that always accompanied her mother's presence pressed its lead weight down on her heart. "This is Victor, my boyfriend. Victor, this is my mother, Cheryl."

"Pleased to meet you, ma'am." He extended his hand.

She touched it for a moment with limp fingers. "Come in. Your sisters are already here." She walked away.

Caroline grimaced. *This isn't going to go well.*

～

They entered the house. Caroline led Victor to the formal living room.

Victor considered what lay before him. He could see it was meant to impress with no thought given to comfort. The sofa that faced the bay window was an antique with a curved back and royal blue velvet upholstery. Angled in the corner sat another antique, a hutch filled with carefully arranged dolls that looked like toys but couldn't be touched. A black armchair sat on either side of the sofa, and little glass and wood tables between appeared too fragile to set a cup on.

Three adults perched on the uncomfortable chairs while four children sipped cocoa from Styrofoam cups on the floor.

"Angelica, Meredith, hi." Caroline greeted her sisters.

"Caroline!" The ladies rose to their feet and scooped her into a tight hug. One had dark hair, like hers, the other blond, like their mother. "We've missed you. Thanksgiving was a flat bore without you," the blond said.

Caroline looks like a child between their imposing heights, Victor noted with an irreverent grin.

"Sorry. I had other plans." Caroline shot Victor a naughty look.

His grin turned into a smirk. *What a feast we shared.* He stuffed his hands into his pockets to deal with his inopportune reaction to the memory.

"And who is this?" asked the brunette, eying him without judgment.

"This is my boyfriend. Victor, these are my sisters. Angelica," she patted the blond, "and Meredith. And," she indicated a rocking chair in the corner of the room, where a quiet-looking man sat holding a baby, "this is Meredith's husband Frank."

Victor shook hands with each adult, reviewing the names and observing the family groupings.

"Meredith and Frank have three kids: Lizzy, Margot and baby Charlie," Caroline explained, indicating two big kids who looked like their parents, with dark hair and pale skin. They could easily have been Caroline's. The baby on his father's shoulder resembled his sisters as much as a drooling, toothless little old man could.

Caroline continued. "These are Angelica's children, Daniel and Julie." These middle-elementary aged kids did not resemble their cousins. Clearly, their father was African-American. Both kids had the attractive medium-brown coloring and thick dark hair that marked them as biracial. Angelica wore a bold wedding ring.

"Pleased to meet all of you," he said in his softest, shyest voice. *I wish I could be confident; these seem like nice folks, but this oppressive atmosphere is killing me.* His eyes met Frank's and he recognized a fellow shy man. They grinned at each other.

"Have some cider," Angelica said, offering a cup to Victor. He took it gratefully and escorted Caroline to the sofa. The stiff blue upholstery refused comfort, but they perched anyway.

Everyone looked around the room, wondering who would speak next. The silence stretched out.

"So, Victor," Cheryl said finally, "what do you do?"

"He's an engineer," Caroline told her mother quickly.

An engineer, not a student? It's not a lie, but almost. I wonder what's up with that. Hmmm.

Cheryl nodded, softening a fraction. "Ah. That's a good profession."

"Yes. It's interesting," he told her.

Apparently, the exchange had loosened her tongue. "I won't lie to you, Victor. I'm rather disappointed."

"At what, ma'am," he asked, though from earlier conversations he expected he knew.

"At you being here. Caroline used to have a boyfriend I liked very much. I can't imagine why they broke things off."

Just as I thought… but how the hell do I answer that?

"Well, mother," Caroline interceded again, a hard note in her voice and her eyes pinched at the corners. "I'll explain if you like. First of all, he never wanted to get married or have children, and you know how much those things mean to me. Second, he was unfaithful."

"Unfaithful?" Cheryl turned wide eyes on her daughter.

Interesting that she moves her face as little as possible. Must be trying to avoid wrinkles. The unkind thought caused Victor a pang of guilt and he struggled to reign in his unruly thoughts.

"Yes. He was having an affair with another woman right under my nose," Caroline explained, shooting apologetic glances at her sisters.

Cheryl rolled her eyes. "So? Men often have their peccadilloes. For a man of William's distinction, wouldn't it have been worthwhile to overlook it?"

"I don't think so. I'm much happier now." Caroline squeezed Victor's hand.

He ran his thumb over her fingers. "Um, what does everyone else do?" he asked, hoping to divert the conversation away from himself.

"I teach second grade," Angelica said, "at Wilder elementary."

Victor raised his eyebrows. *Wilder is a school in a*

rough neighborhood, the students mostly low income and the property values low. "That must be… rewarding," he said.

She beamed. "It is. I just love it there."

"Sounds like teaching runs in the family," he commented.

"It does." Frank piped up, "I teach social studies at Central High School."

"What subject?" Victor asked, capitalizing on the easing of the tension to keep the ball rolling.

"World History, regular and A.P."

"I took A.P. World History," Victor replied. "That class was tough."

Frank nodded. "That's for sure. It just keeps getting tougher. The kids really rise to it though. I love it that I can teach them to think and make connections. That's important in preparing them for college."

"Yes," Caroline agreed. "You don't know how many students arrive at the university not being able to think critically. Those who can quickly rise to the top. You make a difference every day, Frank."

He beamed.

So did Victor. *It never ceases to amaze me how sweet Caroline is to everyone.*

"I," Meredith said, "am currently on maternity leave, but normally I teach music at Walker Middle School."

"Wow, this really is an educational family," Victor observed.

"Well, Dad's a teacher," Meredith said. "It must be in our blood."

Cheryl made a face. "My father was a banker. How I wish my children had chosen that noble profession."

The adults looked one to another, each daring the other to start things up again, but no one spoke.

Who would, after our entire roomful of dreams, goals and vocations have been shot to hell with a single sentence?

The baby began to fuss, and Meredith rose and

scooped him out of her husband's arms saying, "I hope you will all excuse me for a few minutes."

She walked out of the room.

"Disgusting," Cheryl said, her face sourer than ever.

Weird. I didn't see anything disgusting. I wonder what she's talking about.

The conversation died. It became too hard to keep it going in the face of Cheryl's disapproval. Everyone squirmed awkwardly, wondering what to say next, until Angelica's daughter scurried over to her mother and said, "Mommy, can we please watch television now?"

"I suppose," Angelica replied. "Come on, kiddos." She collected her children and Meredith's and led the way, like the Pied Piper, out of the room. Caroline stood and followed, bringing Victor with her.

In the den, they found Meredith sitting in a brown leather rocking chair. She had propped her feet up on a round tufted footstool with a blanket draped over her. As she nursed the baby, she sang softly to him.

Angelica turned on the television and quickly found "How the Grinch Stole Christmas." The kids cheered and settled themselves on the plush tan carpet.

Victor smiled as he led Caroline to a flowered loveseat. *The environment in this little room already feels much nicer.*

"How are you holding up?" she asked him softly.

"Okay," he replied, though in truth he felt a bit raw, as though steel wool had been rubbed on his insides. "How did you guys survive with your personality and sense of humor intact?"

"We left the nest as quickly as possible," Angelica told him, "and we rarely come back. This and Thanksgiving are about it, and I don't even always do that."

"Why not?" he asked. "If I went more than a week or two without visiting my folks, there would be hell to pay."

"Let me ask you this," Angelica demanded, hands

on hips. "If your mother refused to let your spouse come and visit, how often would you do it?"

Victor stared, appalled. "She what?"

Angelica sighed. "Yes. Lucas is black, so Mom won't let him in the house."

He let out a disgusted huff. "I'm surprised you come at all."

"I come to see Caroline and Meredith," Angelica explained. "I wouldn't be surprised, Victor, if she does the same to you, being as how you've replaced that moron Caroline used to go out with."

"No one liked him, did they?" Caroline asked sheepishly.

"Sweetie, *you* didn't even like him," Angelica retorted. "I'm glad to see you've stopped settling."

"Yes." She snuggled closer to Victor and he wrapped his arm around her. "Hey, now that I have you two alone, I have something great to tell you."

"What's that?" Meredith asked, awkwardly switching the baby to her other breast under the blanket.

"I'm pregnant." She beamed.

Both sisters gawked at her, astonished.

"Wow," Angelica finally said. "Um, congratulations... but isn't it kind of fast?"

"Maybe, but who cares?" She settled her hand on Victor's thigh. He covered it with his own.

"I'm glad for you," Meredith told her. "I know waiting for this has been driving you crazy."

"Uh-huh. I'm over the moon." She beamed.

"I bet. Boy, is Mom going to be pissed." Meredith had settled the baby and returned to rocking.

"Why?" Victor asked.

"Well, apart from the fact that she really doesn't like children," Meredith explained, "it's going to kill her that she has to put up with even more family members who aren't fully white. I can't wait to see the fireworks when she figures out you're Hispanic."

"Meredith, stop," her sister protested. "You're freaking me out." Caroline's hand tightened on Victor's.

"What did you expect, Caroline?" Angelica demanded, stroking her daughter's dark, curly hair. "You know how she feels."

"I know," Caroline admitted, biting her lower lip and feigning bravado, "but being with Victor is the best thing that's ever happened to me. I refuse to feel bad about it."

"No, of course not," Meredith assured her. "You're glowing. I've never seen you so happy. I'm glad for you. You know race doesn't bother me. All that matters is that you're happy and he treats you well."

"No one in this room will judge you, certainly," Angelica added, "but you know what's going to happen."

Caroline sighed. "Isn't there a better way for us to get together? I want to have fun with my sisters and their families. This is not fun."

"There is a way," Victor said, drawing everyone's attention. *Oops. Look what happens when I open my mouth!*

His beloved turned to him with started, wide eyes. "What do you mean?"

Victor drew in a deep breath. "Next year, let's have a family Christmas party at our house. It's big enough. And everyone can be invited. Your husband, Angelica, and what about your dad and his family? Your mom can be invited too."

"She won't come, not if Lucas is there," Angelica reminded them.

"Won't that be better?" Meredith demanded. "Then we could enjoy our time together instead of trembling in terror."

"You don't mind, do you, Caroline?" Victor asked.

"No, that's great!" she exclaimed, beaming at him and warming his heart and cheeks in one gesture. "I

177

never thought of it, but you're right. Coming here is tradition, but that doesn't mean it's necessary."

"Right," Angelica agreed. "Brilliant."

Meredith nodded.

"Victor, you're a genius." Caroline kissed him softly on the lips. "Well, Meredith, we'd better go rescue your husband," Caroline said with a sigh. "He's been alone with the dragon for too long already."

They trooped out, leaving Meredith and the children to watch television.

~

When they returned to the living room, Frank sat alone, a look of relief plastered across his face.

"Where did Mom go?" Caroline asked him.

"To check on the dinner," he replied, dragging one knuckle across his forehead. "Whew."

*I hope she wasn't mean to him. Normally she pretends he's not here. Rather than embarrass the shy man—Victor has taught me so much about what goes on beneath the surface—*she commented, "Oh. Is it turkey as usual?"

"Smells like it." He wrinkled his nose.

Caroline frowned. *She sacrificed it again. Ugh. It's not that hard to cook a turkey.* "I'd better go help." She slid her arms around Victor's neck and kissed him again. Then she headed resignedly down the hall.

Like the living room, the kitchen had been designed with form rather than function in mind. The marble counters and glass-fronted cabinets existed mostly to display antique china and kitchenware, and to highlight the conspicuously expensive appliances. "Do you need any help, Mom?"

Cheryl glanced up from the counter where she was carving the bird. It crumbled as the knife pressed into the meat. "Yes. Please make some gravy, would you?"

Tradition again. Ugh. Looks like it's my job as usual to

make the turkey edible. She pulled out a whisk and turned on the burner under the turkey drippings.

"So this is the man you've replaced William with?" Cheryl said, a disapproving note in her voice.

"Yes," Caroline replied, refusing to react, but dumping a liberal dose of white wine onto the crusted meat juices. *Burn out fast, alcohol. I need this gravy, or I'll throw up the meat, but don't worry, babies. You're safe. Mama knows what she's doing.*

"Why?" Cheryl demanded.

"I told you why. William was never going to marry me."

"So? I didn't think you cared about that."

Caroline looked away from the bubbling concoction of pinot grigio and stared at her mother. "Are you joking? I've said I did a thousand times."

"Well, your new man doesn't look like much."

She's sneering. An engineer—a handsome, wonderful, tender engineer—and her puckered lips could sour sugar candy.

"He's certainly not distinguished like William."

"He's kind," Caroline retorted. "To me, that's better. Besides, he loves me. William never loved me."

"He would have given you a good life," Cheryl groused.

"He would have given me a broken heart," Caroline shot back, "and possibly a sexually transmitted disease."

Cheryl grimaced at the mention of sex. "Don't be vulgar, Caroline."

"It's a fact, Mother." *With him splitting time between my bed and Jessie the wild child's, it's more likely than not. God, why did I ever tolerate that loser? I'm damned lucky how well everything turned out.*

"And now? How do you know this new man is safer?" Cheryl crossed her arms under her breasts. Her expensive and subtle boob job thrust forward, creating freckled cleavage under the V-neck of her blouse

"Well, it's called honest conversation. It works well." Caroline could hear sarcasm creeping into her voice.

"You can't know he's honest," Cheryl retorted.

"He can't know I am. That's where trust comes in," she reminded her mother. "I've known Victor for ages, and I've always found him to be truthful, unlike William." She shuddered. "I'll probably marry Victor, Mom. You deserve to know." She paused, glanced at her still-flat belly, and added, "We're also expecting."

Cheryl didn't speak, and so Caroline mixed flour into the pan drippings and whisked.

"Has he asked you to marry him?" Cheryl asked once the racket of metal on metal subsided.

"Not yet, but I know he will someday. I can't wait." Despite the tension, Caroline shivered with delight at the thought. *The whole family I wanted. A loving husband. Kids. The works. From disaster to perfection in a few short months. I'm beyond lucky.*

"And who will you be then?" Cheryl demanded.

Caroline poured chicken broth into the roux in the roasting pan and whisked vigorously. *This is it, the critical moment.* She took a deep breath. "I'll be Dr. Caroline Martinez."

"Martinez?" Cheryl turned to face her daughter. Bits of dry turkey fell from the knife and scattered across the black slate floor tiles.

"Yes."

"Is he a Spaniard? He looks like one." Cheryl sounded desperate.

"No. His dad is Mexican." *Take that. Your lessons in racism had no impact on me. Yes, I'm in love with a Mexican man and proud of it.*

Cheryl's eye bugged out. "What? You let... that... touch you?" She sounded nauseated.

"Oh yes." She drew out the words into a lovesick sigh that was only slightly exaggerated.

"How could you do that?"

"He's a good man, and I love him. Why not?" Caroline asked lightly.

This appeared to be the last straw. Cheryl burst out, "Really, Caroline! I can't believe you've been such a slut. I've heard they have a certain... animal appeal, but I thought you were more sophisticated in your tastes."

"Don't say another word, Mom," Caroline warned. "Victor is *not* an animal. He's a good man, an educated, ambitious, intelligent man and he loves me. I would think that would mean something to you."

At that moment, Victor appeared. Of course he did, wrapping his arm around her waist.

She leaned her head against him.

Cheryl shook her head in disgust. "You were my last hope, Caroline. After your sister married that..."

Caroline gave her mother a warning look.

Cheryl glared back but did not complete the slur she had clearly intended to use. "And then Meredith with her shabby little teacher. I had hoped you would have the sense to keep your museum director. He was a real man. And now, here you are with this..." And then she said another word, a terrible word, one that implied that Victor's Mexican grandparents had not entered the country legally.

Victor went rigid. His arm fell away from Caroline in shock.

"Mother, how dare you?" she cried, deeply ashamed, her face hot with anger, her voice loud. "I can't believe you would say such a thing. You know, you appall me. What a disgusting thing to say."

"No, the half breed mongrel you're carrying is disgusting."

"That's your grandchildren you're talking about! I

won't have it. Victor's never done anything to you, you bigot. You apologize!" Caroline yelled.

The raised voices drew the other family members into the room.

"I won't," Cheryl vowed through clenched teeth.

"You'd better reconsider if our relationship means anything to you." Caroline waved a finger in her mother's direction. "I won't listen to my man being put down this way. You will treat him with respect."

Cheryl didn't back down an inch. "It's my house. I'm free to say what I damned well choose."

"And I'm free not to be in it anymore," Caroline shot back. "In fact, I would be very pleased never to come back here again."

"Then go. Get out. Don't come back," Cheryl dared her daughter, gesturing toward the door with a jerk of her head.

"If you're exaggerating, Mother, I'm not. We don't need someone like you in our lives. Come on, Victor. Let's go, baby." She took his hand and led him to the door.

"You know," she heard Angelica saying behind her; "I think Caroline's got the right idea. Why stay where you're unwelcome? Julie, Daniel, let's go." She collected her children and followed them into the night.

As Caroline slammed her car door shut, she saw Frank and Meredith's headlights flare. The uncomfortable tradition of spending Christmas Eve at Mother's house imploded under its own weight, never to be resurrected.

On the drive home, both Caroline and Victor remained silent.

Victor glared as though reacting to darkly unpleasant thoughts.

Caroline shook with fury and embarrassment that choked off her words. All the long way, the silence grew between them.

They had been silent before, but for the first time it felt uncomfortable, and when they got out of the car, Victor didn't touch Caroline. He didn't take her hand, or wrap his arm around her waist, the way he normally did.

Terrified by Victor's unprecedented demeanor, her aimless mental chattering increased. *I don't know this side of him at all and have no idea what it means.* She thought desperately for something—anything—to say that could break the icy stalemate, but not one work could force its way between her tingling lips.

Inside the chilly mudroom, Caroline pulled off her boots and jacket a moment before Victor gripped her arm and escorted her into the formal living room. *We normally sit in the den where it's more comfortable. Why did he bring us here?* Her stomach began clenching immediately.

"Sit down, Caroline," Victor said, his voice cold and hard.

She sat.

He didn't. He remained standing, frowning down at her.

"Victor," she burst out finally, "I'm so sorry about what she said. It was terrible."

"Yes, it was. I hate that racist bullshit." His jaw clenched and she could hear his teeth grinding.

"I know. It wasn't right. You know I don't feel that way," she insisted.

"But you brought me there, knowing how she felt. Why?" he demanded. His fists clenched. For the first time since she met Victor, his wiry muscles looked threatening rather than protective.

"You know why," she retorted, though at the moment she could no longer remember the words to express it.

"You could have invited your sisters over for dinner, met them at a restaurant, anything. This wasn't necessary."

She closed her eyes. "You're right. I didn't think. I didn't realize it would be so bad."

"Oh come on, Caroline," he sneered, "Your brother-in-law isn't even allowed in the house. What the hell did you think was going to happen?"

"I'm sorry. I'm so sorry." Tears welled up in Caroline's eyes and one spilled over, trailing a burning line down her cheek. "I never meant for you to be hurt."

"I'm sorry too."

She looked up, another tear rolling down her face.

He glared at her with the angriest expression she'd ever seen on his face. "Sorry I trusted you. You knew how I felt, you knew how ugly she could be, and you brought me there anyway. That's not how you treat someone you love."

The pain of his words slapped her like a physical blow. Caroline recoiled from it. "I don't know what to tell you. How can I make this right?"

Victor drew himself up to his full height and crossed his arms over his chest. "I don't know if you can. How can I be with someone who comes from… that?"

"That's not me," she pleaded, hearing the desperation in her own voice. "I'm not that way."

"You still seek her out though. You still go to her." His accusation held the weight of attempted murder.

"She's my mother," Caroline protested, "but after tonight, I'm not going anymore."

"It's too late for that now. The damage is done."

"What do you mean?" *Oh, God. Let that not be what it sounds like!*

"I don't know. I have to think about this. It may be too much." He turned away from her.

"Please say you don't mean it," Caroline begged, sobbing as she slunk from the couch and grasped the back of his shirt in her hand. "I need you, Victor."

He shook her off. "You got what you needed from me."

Sobs clawed their way out of Caroline's throat, obliterating thought and speech in one.

He sighed. When he next spoke, his voice sounded a hair less certain, though to Caroline's overwrought emotions, the change was insignificant. "Listen, I'd better not say anything else. I'm too mad. I don't want to do anything I might regret later. I'm leaving."

"Will you come back?" She circled around his body and looked up into his face, her own tear-streaked visage pleading without shame.

"I don't know." He stalked around her and out of the room.

She heard the door slam and his car rev back to life.

Alone in her empty house, Caroline curled up on the couch, holding a pillow to her belly, aching to her very soul. If she had once doubted her love for Victor, she felt none now. *This relationship is not a rebound, not an impulse. He's my heart... and he's gone.*

Losing William had been a minor setback, but she feared losing Victor might prove fatal.

CHAPTER 12

*N*ot knowing what else to do, Victor drove back to his apartment. Striding into the room, he passed the kitchenette along the south wall, so he opened the mini-fridge. Pulling out a bottle of beer, he shuffled over to his shabby sofa and flopped down, still seething.

It had shocked him to the core of his being that Caroline, sweet Caroline who treated everyone with respect, had come from a mother like that Cheryl. No doubt she had listened to that garbage her whole life. *There's no way it wouldn't have had an impact*, he thought bitterly.

The part of Victor that had loved this woman from the first day he walked into her class seven semesters ago ached to reach out to her, to go back and explain, or at least to call, but a cloud of rage squashed down the urge.

He had heard those words before... animal, and worse. Not everyone had been kind to the half-Mexican boy growing up. *Not that I'm ashamed of my heritage. I'm proud of it, damn it, but some people just don't see me as human. It figures Caroline's mother is one of those. When she thought I was an engineer, Cheryl showed a glimmer of approval, but that accomplishment became meaningless in an*

186

instant, just because my grandmother speaks Spanish and my father's skin is brown. I don't know what's next, or what I want, other than to destroy something.

A knock at the door shook him from his angry mental rant. Cursing under his breath, he yanked it open. His mother stood outside, wrapped in an unfastened jacket, her long red hair blowing in the icy December wind. She wore bedroom slippers.

"Mom?" he asked, faking calm while inwardly, he raged.

"Victor, why are you here? What's wrong? Where's Caroline?" she burst out as she stepped over the threshold into the apartment.

Victor didn't back up. *I don't want you either right now, Mom.* "Caroline is at her house. I'm sorry, but I don't really feel like talking." He crossed his arms over his chest and glared, but with his mother, he found himself unable to muster the same conviction he'd felt earlier.

Sam ignored him, pushing her way into the room. "Her house?" she asked her son. "I thought it was your house too. What's going on?"

Victor shook his head vigorously. "It wasn't my house. It never was. I never paid a cent towards it."

She turned to stare at him in confusion. "Not yet, but weren't you going to change that once you graduate?"

He shook his head again. "I don't know. It was the plan, but things change. I don't think I can go back there anymore."

Sam's eyebrows drew together into a confused and angry red line. The grooves around her mouth deepened as her lips pursed. "Not go back? What on earth, son? The woman you've loved for years invited you to live with her, and she's carrying your child. Last week you were talking about marrying her. She's been talking about marrying you all along. Now, suddenly, it's over? How can that be?"

187

SIMONE BEAUDELAIRE

"I don't want to talk about it," Victor repeated himself.

"Humph. You're here in your apartment alone, without the mother of my grandchild, on Christmas Eve. I think you'd better let it out." Sam thought for a moment. "She didn't sleep with someone else, did she?"

Victor blinked in surprise. *Caroline? Sleep with...* "No, nothing like that. Why would you think that?"

"It's the only reason I could think of that you would walk away," Sam said. She crossed her own arms over her chest.

"No."

"Then you'd better tell me what happened," Sam pressed.

"Why?" Victor demanded, cursing when the question emerged as more of a childish whine than a furious roar.

"Because it's tearing you up."

She's right. Victor felt ripped open inside. His soul bled. "What if I told you that Caroline comes from such a terrible family that the thought of ever going near them again makes me physically ill?"

"Hmm." Sam thought for a moment. "That's hard. Is she close to them?"

"Not really," he admitted, sulking. *Just accept it, Mom. If you're going to butt in, accept my explanations.*

Sam insisted on clarification. "Is it the whole family?" she demanded, staring into Victor's eyes, forcing him not to prevaricate or exaggerate.

Victor made himself answer honestly, though he still just wanted to blast. "Actually, no. It's only her mother, Cheryl. The rest of them were okay."

"Ah, a bad mother is hard. I had one too. But you say she's not close to her?" Sam insisted.

"No, but she still goes back to visit a couple of times a year." *Damn, that sounds stupid when I say it out loud. Please, just go, Mom. Leave me alone.*

188

Sam, of course, did no such thing. She'd gotten the bit in her teeth and there was no stopping her now. "And that makes you want to leave her why?" she challenged her son.

"You can't imagine what that woman just said to me," Victor mumbled.

"What?"

Victor struggled to choke out the words Cheryl had said.

Sam's jaw sagged and a look of horrified sympathy creased her face. She threw her arms around her son and hugged him tight, rubbing his back soothingly the way she had done when he was a child. "How terrible. I'm so sorry," she gushed. "No wonder you're angry. You have every right to be. That it came from Caroline's mother is even worse."

See, I'm not being dramatic, he thought. *She understands.*

Sam continued, releasing her son to regard his face. "But I'm confused about something. You sound like your madder at Caroline than at Cheryl. Did she agree with what her mother was saying? I can hardly believe she would, given that she chose you to be the father of her child."

"No," he admitted.

"What did she say?"

Victor sighed. *This isn't going the way I want. I don't want fact and reason. I want to blow up and be mad.* "She told her mother off good, yelled at her."

"Caroline yelled?" Sam's eyes widened. She looked as though she couldn't believe such a thing.

A tiny thread of admiration flared to life in the midst of Victor's anger. "Oh yes. Called her a bigot, said she was appalled and demanded that she apologize, and treat me with respect. Cheryl refused, so we left. Caroline told her mother she wouldn't be back. I think she started a chain reaction because her sisters left at that time too. I guess everyone had had enough."

"Well, it sounds like she did the right thing," Sam replied, laying it on the line. "She defended you, didn't she?"

He nodded.

"Defended you to her own mother," she added, in case he'd missed the point.

"Yes."

"Then what are you mad at her about? It sounds like you should be proud of her."

Damn it, now Mom sounds mad, and not at Caroline, or even Cheryl. Victor bit the inside of his cheek. "She brought me there," he snapped, attempting to justify his anger. "She knew her mother hates... non-Europeans. Her sister's husband is black, and he never gets to come over. She told me ahead of time that her mother would never accept me because I'm Mexican. I told her that I wasn't comfortable meeting someone like that, but she wanted me to get to know her sisters and asked me to ignore it as if anyone could ignore that."

Sam nodded. "That might have been asking a lot. Still... her mother. It's hard to stop wanting your mother's approval, even when you know you're not going to get it. After all, you were quick to bring Caroline here."

"Yes," Victor shot back, dismayed by the unfounded comparison, "but there was no risk there. I knew you would love her."

"And we do," Sam assured him, her narrowed eyes demanding he understand the full implications of that love. "So does your grandmother, but Caroline didn't know that."

"And she *did* know that her mother wouldn't like me. She shouldn't have suggested it," Victor groused.

Sam's eyebrows raised, transforming her forehead into the image of a pale, plowed field. "Victor, you're not making sense. Introducing the person you love to your family is a natural step. She wanted to show you off to them, make them see how proud she is of you. Her mother's difficulty didn't make her want to hide you. She loves you more than she fears her mother's prejudice. It's a compliment."

"It doesn't feel like one." Victor sulked, cringing at his childish tone.

"I suppose not," Sam conceded, "and if you want to be angry with Cheryl, you're entitled. I don't think you can legitimately be angry with Caroline. She made a miscalculation with the best of intentions."

"You know what they say about intentions," he snapped, clinging to his anger by the threads left to him.

Sam sighed and patted his shoulder. "Yes. But you don't really think she was trying to hurt you, do you? I've rarely seen a woman so in love as Caroline is with you."

His mother's words stung. "I don't know that she really loves me all that much," he snapped.

Sam's lips turned down in a disbelieving frown. "Why? Because of this one mistake today?"

Victor dug deep for the half-truth with which he'd been justifying his defection. "No, I think she's grateful to me for helping her conceive, and she enjoys my attention and she's confusing that with love. She's never been loved by a man before."

Sam dismissed his reasoning with a sharp waving motion and a disbelieving snort. "No, I disagree. It's you. It's not the baby thing, not entirely. I mean, you know women can get a baby without a man if they really want to."

"Yes." *I do know that*, he added silently, remembering the contributions he'd made over the years.

"So if Caroline wanted a baby, she could have purchased the means," Sam pressed on, going in for the kill. "She's a professor. I'm sure she could have afforded it, but that's not what happened, is it?"

191

"No." He tried not to remember, but vivid images of Caroline's sweet body twined around him insisted on crowding into his mind.

"Is she a woman who goes to bed with men easily?" Sam probed for information. Her tone held no judgment. "Is she like the one you dated before?"

"No. Other than me, she's only had one relationship, and they were together three years. She said she made him wait a whole year too." *Why did I admit that?*

Sam's expression turned triumphant. "Ah. And how long did she make you wait, I mean, once you two decided to go beyond the teacher and student relationship?"

"About ten seconds," Victor admitted, momentarily losing the thread of the conversation in a flurry of tender and sexy memories. He forced his attention back to his mother.

"So, this cautious woman, who's never given her heart, who's very hesitant about sharing her body, gave you both within... about two weeks?"

"I suppose. What point are you trying to make, Mom?" he asked, frantically searching his mind for his next counter-argument. His ammunition had grown painfully thin.

Sam's expression told him it should be obvious. "That she must really trust you and think you're incredibly special. I mean, she chose you to be the father of her child, even though she's surrounded by professors, even though the means can also be discretely purchased, saving her from committing herself at all. She had options. She chose you to be her lover instead, risking her heart to be with you so the two of you could make a family for your child."

As his anger drained away, Victor's guilt welled up.

"What?" Sam demanded, reading his expression.

"She risked more than that. She had trouble at work because of our relationship. I think she almost got fired. Certainly, her professional reputation has suffered."

Sam raised one eyebrow. "And how did that affect your relationship?"

"It didn't." He scrubbed his hand over his face. "She said she wanted to work less after... the delivery anyway. She wanted me to provide for her."

"I imagine you found that idea appealing," Sam stated baldly.

"Yes."

Sam glared at him until he squirmed, but like an insect pinned to a board, he could not escape her penetrating stare. "I can't believe that you would leave someone who has risked so much for you, someone you've wanted so long, because her mother—who you say she isn't close to anyway—said some ugly things," Sam told him, not giving him the slightest opportunity to interject a word.

Her tirade continued. "That wasn't Caroline's fault, and it's clear she doesn't agree. Never forget how nice she was to your family, how she dredged up as much Spanish as she could remember to introduce herself to your grandmother. Okay, it was a mistake for her to introduce you to her mother, but Victor, it was Cheryl, not Caroline, who said... *that*. Be angry at the person who hurt you, not just the one who's convenient."

She paused again, but he made no attempt to interrupt. "I suppose since you knew Cheryl wouldn't care about your opinion, and you would never be able to tell her how you felt, you lashed out at the next available person. I can understand how you lost control, but don't make it more than it was. You know there are bigots in the world, and I'm sure it hurts like hell to meet one face to face, but it only tells us something is lacking in her. It doesn't mean there's anything wrong with you. And don't make it Caroline's problem. I'm sure she's upset enough already."

Victor, busy digesting the information, didn't reply.

"Sounds like maybe you didn't love her that much yourself," Sam snapped.

The words cut through Victor's contemplations and shook him to the core. "Mom, you know better than that."

"Do I?" Sam scowled at her son and he winced. "Have you treated her like a real person? Or did you just see her as a means to fulfill a fantasy? You're hardly the first young man to dream about a pretty teacher. Is that what this was? You wanted her, and she was willing because she wanted a baby, so she let you make love to her. She's a real person, Victor. She has baggage; issues and vulnerabilities like anyone else. Did you really think she wouldn't? That her sole reason for existing would be to let you live out your fantasies?"

"Of course not. Caroline is like no one I've ever met. She's special."

Sam pressed on. "If you love her so much, then let her be a little conflicted. Let her struggle with giving up a difficult mother. She's thinking a lot about motherhood right now. It's a time when a woman naturally wants her mother's support. She isn't going to get it. Don't hate her for trying, son. Be honest. Isn't she worth more to you than this? You made her fall in love with you. You made her pregnant. What's your baby going to do if you're gone?"

Lost again in his own ruminations, Victor corrected his mother without thought. "Babies not baby."

"Say that again." Sam's voice dropped to an intense quiet.

Realizing he'd given himself away, Victor admitted, "Babies. Caroline found out last week that it's twins."

This time Sam lost control. "Two babies?" she shouted. "She's pregnant with two babies? And you walked away? Oh my God, Victor, how could you do that? You can't imagine how vulnerable a pregnant woman is, how hard it is to carry a child. It must be even harder with two. She's in an incredibly fragile state. She was depending on you, and you left her." She shook her head. "I'm not very proud of you right now, son."

"But, Mom..." he began, and then shut his mouth with a snap, realizing he had no argument to offer.

"Yes, I know you're hurting, but think about it. You're hurting because a stranger, who will never be part of your life again, said something... okay, something really wrong and terrible. That you're upset about it is natural, but think of how much more Caroline must be hurting now, knowing her own mother hurt the man she loves so much, he walked away leaving her pregnant and alone. I think she must be about destroyed. Picture it, son. What do you think she's doing right now?"

"Sleeping?" he suggested.

Sam gave him a sour look. "Not a chance. You know the answer. She's crying, heartbroken because, despite all your words of passionate love, you didn't love her enough to forgive a simple mistake. She wanted her family to know you because she loves you and it all blew up in her face."

Victor did picture it. *Mom's right. I hurt Caroline as much as I was hurt.* He remembered her, trembling with shock and pain, tears streaming down her face as he departed.

How could I have gone from wanting to marry her to walking out the door in one evening? I pushed my love on Caroline until she felt safe to love me back, and it was disingenuous to imply she didn't. I swore she could trust me, that I would never hurt her, and then I lashed out horrendously, calling into question all the sweetness of the last month and making a lie of the years I desired her. Was I really using her after all because she's so pretty and I wanted to have sex with her?

His heart howled in protest at the ridiculousness of the thought, finally cutting through his rage and forcing him to see what he'd lost.

No. That can't be. The sex was phenomenal, but I truly wanted more. He thought again about how he had left her, weeping, cut deep in her heart from his attack, and the last vestiges of his rage collapsed. *How could I have thrown away something so precious?* He raised burning eyes to his mother. "What can I do?"

"You can't undo what's been done. This hurt will be part of your relationship forever, but maybe you can get past it. Get your ass back there, right now. Tell her you're sorry, that you don't blame her for what her mother said, and that it was a mistake to blame her at all. Then you do everything you can to help her forget the hurt and remember why she loves you. Actually, you know one thing you can do to fix it. Do you still have what I gave you?"

He patted his pocket. "Yes."

"Give it to her. That will definitely help."

"Will she let me come back?" he asked, no longer caring that he sounded like a wheedling child.

"I don't know. You've screwed up pretty bad. You can only try… and pray."

Victor raced out the door.

CHAPTER 13

*C*aroline moved from the sofa to her bed. It took ages to make her way down the hall and up the stairs. Her whole body felt like it had been beaten. She hurt from head to toe, most of all her heart. The terrible agony quickly turned to nausea, which was the only thing that had gotten her out of the living room at all. She threw up until there was nothing left in her stomach, and then dry heaved afterwards. Finally, empty and drained, she brushed her teeth and shuffled down the hall to her bedroom, shedding her dress on the floor.

Rumpled covers from this morning, when Victor and I made love. It was so sweet. Tears clawed their way out of her burning eyes and she sank onto the mattress. *He was the best lover a woman could ask for; tender, passionate and wonderfully skilled. Will I really never hold him close again?* Choked with broken sobs, she buried her face in a pillow, and there she remained, weeping until her phone rang. She stared at the buzzing box, wondering if it mattered. *It might be Victor. I have to try.* She lifted the phone listlessly and looked at the display screen. Angelica. She pushed the button and held it to her ear.

"Hello?" she choked out.

"Caroline?"

She couldn't answer.

"Are you there?"

"Uh-huh." She sobbed.

"Wow, you sound really bad," her sister commented. "Are you okay?"

"No. I'm terrible."

"Yeah, she was really out of line."

"I can't believe she actually said... that." The words emerged as hesitant whimpers.

"Caroline, she says things like that all the time. Do you want to know what her pet name for Lucas is? I'll give you a hint. It starts with an N."

Caroline's jaw dropped. Her sister's blunt admission momentarily stunned her from her tears. "Why do you put up with it?" she demanded.

Angelica sighed. "I don't know. I shouldn't. I won't anymore. Lucas loves me more than she ever did. I owe him a big apology."

Caroline nodded, though she knew her sister couldn't see. "Victor loved me more in the past month than she ever did. I'll never forgive her. He was so hurt, so upset. She just cost me the love of my life."

"What?" Angelica demanded, disbelieving.

"He left me." Forcing out the words destroyed her ability to think, and she wept into the phone, trying to muffle the speaker.

"Oh, Caroline," Angelica said when she could finally be heard. "I'm so sorry. And you're pregnant too. Poor baby. What will you do?"

"I don't know. I just want to curl up and die. I've never hurt this badly in my life."

"If there's anything Lucas and I can do, please tell us. No one wanted you to be hurt."

"I don't know. I..." She grabbed a tissue from the bedside table and blew her nose. "It's twins, Angelica. Victor gave me twins. How can I take care of them without him?" Panic threatened, and with it, a new wave of nausea rose into her throat, but her empty belly could only twist and churn.

"Oh, honey, that's so hard," her sister said softly. "Maybe he'll get over it and come back?"

Despair coiled around her like a serpent, constricting tighter with every dark thought. "Why would he? I shouldn't be surprised. We've done everything wrong. I should have guessed it wouldn't last, especially not in the face of... of Mom."

"What do you mean you've done everything wrong?" her sister demanded.

"Everything everyone says about relationships, we did the opposite," she admitted in a painful whimper. "We've broken every taboo. I'm older than him. I had just broken up with my boyfriend of three years. He's a college student. I'm a teacher. I used to be his teacher. We had sex right away, moved in together a week later. I should have known I would screw this up. It was too much, too soon."

Angelica made a dismissive sound. "That doesn't necessarily mean it was hopeless. There was a reason you moved so fast. Both of you wanted it that way." She growled "I'm furious with him. Naturally, he was upset, but to leave? A real man doesn't act that way."

"No, don't blame him. It was too much to ask of anyone, Angelica. We all knew what would happen and I brought him anyway. I'm the one to blame..." Caroline squeaked in surprise as the phone was pulled from her hand.

"Angelica, Caroline will call you back tomorrow." Victor's voice sounded rough and harsh, as though with overwhelming emotion.

"No, you don't, Victor Martinez!" Angelica screeched loud enough for Caroline to hear her. "If you hang up this phone, I'm calling the police!"

"Why?" he asked. Through her haze of tears, Caroline could see bewilderment on his face.

"Swear to me you're not going to hurt her," her sister's voice rang out loud with fear for her.

"No," Victor replied, intensity burning in his eyes and tone. "That's not why I'm here."

"Then why?"

"To fix it." He swallowed hard.

"Do you love her?" Angelica demanded.

"Yes." The burn in his dark eyes revealed his words as true.

"All right then, but she'd better call me at eight tomorrow morning. You understand? Eight a.m. on the dot."

"Yes, ma'am."

He pushed the button and dropped the phone on the table. Then he knelt beside the bed, cupping Caroline's face in his hands. His expression remained frighteningly intense, but he held her tenderly.

She looked up into his eyes, beautiful brown eyes, filled with regret and fear.

"Caroline, I…"

She wrapped her arms around his neck and pulled him down, taking that bewitching mouth with hers and kissing him hard. She could taste her own tears as they ground their mouths together.

They began to make love almost without thought. Sex was such a fundamental part of their relationship, had been from the beginning. It was how they had connected, gotten comfortable together, celebrated each other. It felt natural now, in a moment of extreme distress, to reach for the comfort of each other's bodies.

Victor urged Caroline down onto the bed, leaning over her, their mouths fused in a complex kiss formed of equal parts regret, apology, and plea.

She understood it all, accepted it all and urged him even closer.

He climbed onto the bed, straddling her.

She pulled him down so his body pressed against

hers and held him so tight, not really believing he was there.

He lowered the covers to bare her breasts, nodding in approval at finding her nude. He cupped her in one hand, molding the soft flesh. The tender globe had already grown bigger, swollen with her pregnancy. He released her mouth, touching his lips to her chin, trailing down her throat to take her nipples, one after the other, teasing the points with his tongue.

It hurt. Caroline's breasts were sore, and Victor's mouth on them hurt almost as much as it pleased her, but it didn't matter. *Not when he's here. He came back. He's with me again; he's making love to me.*

She lifted his sweater, pulling it over his head and stroking his bare back. His skin felt silky beneath her fingers.

He lifted his head. "I'm sorry."

"I understand. I'm just glad you're back."

"I don't want to be anywhere else, ever again," he vowed, and the words soothed her.

"I want you somewhere else."

Agony flared in his eyes. "Where?"

"In here." She pushed the covers off herself, parting her thighs wide. Then she cupped her own mound, showing him.

He sucked in a breath. "Oh God."

"Hurry, baby."

Victor tore off his jeans and underwear and took her eager invitation, easing through the drenched, swollen folds, seeking and finding the entrance to her body and gliding into her. They arched together, needing complete penetration, and sighing with relief when they finally reached it.

"Now you're right where you need to be," she murmured.

He kissed her again as he began to thrust into her,

comforting her with sweet loving as he kissed away her tears. "I love you, Caroline."

She closed her eyes. *If Victor left me, I would never have the courage to try to love again. I would die alone. But he came back to me, he forgave me.* She snuggled in his embrace as he pleasured her with deep, deep thrusts, taking her to a glorious peak and making her cry out in delight. Her back bowed, pressing her body up against him.

~

Victor rose up, his hands under her hips, positioning her as he plundered her, so he could watch her squirm on the sheets. *Sweet Caroline, enjoy every moment.* Every drive of his sex into her body carried his love. Every thrust seemed to coax new spasms from her until the hot, wet clenching of her sex stimulated Victor beyond his ability to hold back. With a groan, he gave her his own release.

Then he rolled to his side, sliding out of her body and pulling her tight into his arms. She cuddled against him.

He brushed his hand over her cheek. "There are so many things I need to say to you, I don't even know where to start," he told her.

"You don't have to," she insisted.

"I'm sorry. I overreacted."

She shook her head. "You didn't. It really was that terrible."

His lips compressed. "Yes. It was and she is. I don't want her to be a part of my life—of our life together—but that was no reason for me to question what we have. Especially given how decisively you put her in her place."

Fresh tears welled in her eyes, but her expression spoke only of relief. "It's okay. You came back. That's the important part. You came back right away." She rested her cheek on his shoulder.

"Yeah, I might have tried staying mad a little longer," he admitted wryly, "but Mom told me I was being stupid. She was right."

"Your mom usually is. I really do love her," Caroline admitted with a watery sniffle.

"I'm glad," he replied. "Not everyone would."

Caroline moved her head against his shoulder in what felt like a nod, but when she spoke, she moved the conversation forward, to the place he had not known how to find. "I forgive you, Victor. Do you forgive me?"

He cupped her cheek. "Yes. Of course."

"I love you."

"I love you too."

She kissed his chest.

He petted her back. *A woman's forgiveness is as sweet as her love. Thank you for not holding this against me, little teacher.* But he knew the hurt still existed inside her. *Let's see if I can erase more of it.* "Caroline?"

"Yes, baby?"

"Do you remember the other day, the last day of the semester, when you were so exhausted?"

She considered. "Yes. I remember," she said at last. "We talked about that situation at work."

"Yes, but right before you fell asleep, you said something else. Do you remember?"

She thought again, but it seemed she hadn't been awake after all. "What did I say?"

"You said… you said you wished we could get married."

Her face moved against his shoulder, forming expressions he couldn't see. "Did I?" she mumbled. "I don't remember that. I must have already been asleep."

"Well, at any rate, did you mean it?"

"Huh? Victor, just say what you mean. I'm not following."

"Oh hell. Never mind. Caroline, little teacher, will you marry me?"

Caroline's head shot up, and she blinked in surprise. "What?"

"Marry me, Caroline. Please, baby," he begged.

"Oh, yes. Of course."

"Yes?" *Can it really be this simple?*

"Yes. Isn't that what this has always been about?"

"You're so right. It has. You don't think it's too soon?"

She shook her head. "No. Not at all."

"I don't know how or when we're going to do this, but I do have something for you." He reached over the side of the bed and grabbed his jeans, fumbling in the pocket. Then he took her left hand and slid a ring onto her finger. "It's not a real engagement ring. I can't afford that right now, so I asked Mom to make something for you."

∽

Caroline studied her hand. The ring, made from two parallel loops of gold wire, had a pattern of random scrolling lines and a pink pearl. It must have taken an impossibly tiny tool to make such intricate loops. "Oh, it's so pretty, Victor. Why on earth would you say it's not a real engagement ring?"

"It's not a diamond," he said, as though that explained everything.

"So? Don't have such a one-track mind. You're not an engineer yet. Are we really engaged?"

"Yes."

"Then it's a real engagement ring. Diamonds are kind of obvious, don't you think? This is better. I mean, your mother made it. She doesn't even believe in marriage, but she made this for us. That's incredibly special."

One side of his mouth turned up in a grin. "Yeah. When I asked her to make it, she told me she'd never looked at marriage in the way you described it to her. It made her glad we were together. She always knew I would want to marry someday. She's just happy it's you. She absolutely loves you." His eyes turned from her face to her hand. "She also said something about this ring I don't understand. She told me you would explain it to me. She said this ring represents the three greatest virtues. What does that mean?"

Caroline looked at the ring closely.

"Well, in the Bible it says, 'these three remain; faith, hope, and love, but the greatest of these is love.' I wonder if that's what she means. You know, this pearl could represent the letter O." She peered at the ring, and then a wordless cry escaped her lips. "Look, Victor." With the tip of one finger, she traced the word love, in cursive, twisted diagonally into the wire, with the pearl, as she had thought, representing the o.

He squinted. "I see it."

"Okay." She twisted the ring to one side and, now that she knew what she was looking for, quickly identified the word faith, running beside love. A check of the other side of the ring revealed the word hope.

"She knew you would get it," he informed her with pride.

"It represents us; you know?" Caroline looked up from admiring the ring to meet Victor's eyes.

"How?"

"You hoped I would love you someday if you loved me long enough. You were right."

His expression softened to tenderness. "You held onto hope that you would have a baby, and you had faith I would take care of you."

"And of course, we love each other."

"Of course." They leaned together for a long and lingering kiss.

A yawn shattered the embrace. "Victor?"

"Yes, love?"

"I'm really tired, but I know I won't be able to sleep without you beside me."

"I'm beside you. I'm not going anywhere. Go to sleep. I love you." He kissed her temple. Turning off the lamp, he pulled her close in his arms and stroked her until she drifted into slumber.

CHAPTER 14

$\mathscr{T}$he weeks passed swiftly with so much to plan, and on the first Saturday of Spring Break, at four in the afternoon, a large group of people converged on Victor and Caroline's house: First Sophie arrived, with Brett and their children, then Michael and Sheridan, wearing matching gold bands. Sheridan—also expecting—was due only a week after Caroline, though her belly was considerably smaller.

Maggie brought Jan, whose fiancé visa had finally been approved. Selene arrived at the same time as them, along with her husband Brandon, holding hands and generally behaving like the newlyweds they were, their infant son cradled against his father's shoulder.

Caroline's own dad came, with his wife and their little ones, and of course, Angelica and Lucas, Meredith and Frank, and their families. Children of all ages filled the room.

Sam and Rafael were also there, naturally, with Victor's *abuela*. Seventeen adults and ten children packed into the formal living room.

Located in the corner of Caroline's house, one wall consisted entirely of windows that overlooked the still-frozen lake. A fireplace with a pretty red-brick brick hearth dominated the adjoining wall. A fire crackled cheerfully in honor of the occasion. The large red-flow-ered sectional, which normally sat in the middle of the room, had been pushed back to free up space. Victor and his father had taken the brown leather sofa and loveseat from the den and placed them in front of the window, to form a U with the sectional, and finally, with four armchairs, two at either end, there were seats for all the adults. The decorative pillows had been placed on the floor in front, and the children sat on them.

With Sam's help, two end tables had been positioned flanking the fireplace, covered in red tablecloths over-laid with white lace runners. Each one had an arrange-ment of branches and flowers she had made for the occasion. One table held the guest book, the other the unity candle. A red and white kissing bough had been hung from the ceiling above.

Leave it to Sam to contribute something pagan and beau-tiful, Caroline thought with a smile. *We'll be kissing under it, for sure.*

There was no aisle to walk down, but it didn't mat-ter. Caroline and Victor simply stood together in front of the fireplace, where the officiant waited.

Caroline adjusted her long black maternity skirt and smoothed her hands over a red blouse shot through with gold threads.

"Dearly beloved," the officiant began, "we are gath-ered here today to witness the marriage of Victor and Caroline…"

The brief but pretty ceremony consisted of a mixture of tradition and innovation, and Rafael, seated next to his mother, translated everything into Spanish for her, so she wouldn't be left out. It lasted less than fifteen minutes, so short that only the smallest children began to wiggle. Victor and Caroline exchanged real wedding bands, a gift from Victor's father.

Victor touched his lips to Caroline's and the cere-mony ended. The assembled guests clapped and cheered. Then the parents escorted the kids to the den to watch a movie while a photojournalism major from the university took pictures. It was just the right kind of wedding for a couple like them, and they beamed with satisfaction.

EPILOGUE

$\mathscr{C}$aroline lay sound asleep.

No surprise there, Victor concluded, studying the dark circles under her eyes. Her face looked unnaturally pale. *Delivering twins is no small task. I'm so glad she managed to avoid the cesarean delivery just as she had hoped, but it took every ounce of strength she possessed, and she drew heavily on mine as well.*

Exhaustion clawed at him as he perched on the edge of the hospital bed, but he ignored it. He much preferred to look into the face of his son, cradled in his hands. "Joaquín Rafael Martinez," he whispered. "Hola, mijito. Soy tu papá." He touched his lips to the little boy's forehead.

Joaquin regarded him quietly with baby-gray eyes that would surely turn brown in the end.

It appears another shy Martinez boy has entered the world. Victor grinned. "You look so tiny to me. Barely six pounds." He smoothed a wisp of dark hair with his fingertips. "The doctors say you're a marvelous size... for a twin. Must be because your mother took such good care of herself—and you and your sister—leading up to delivery. Your sister has a good three ounces on you, but she still looks too small to be real."

He glanced over to the rocking chair nearby. There,

Sam cradled his daughter against her shoulder, patting her little back.

A myriad of images blended with the sight of his children, playing across Victor's mind like a movie, and he narrated the events to Joaquin in an undertone.

"You won't understand this for a long time, but I just graduated from college." He smiled tiredly at the memory. "Even from my seat among the graduates, I could see how difficult it was for your mama to waddle up the steps and find her seat among the other faculty. You two were so big in her belly by then. Dr. Burke—he wants me to call him Michael now, which seems weird—and his wife helped her into her seat. Sheridan Murphy-Burke is a really nice lady. I guess their baby must be due any day now. Maybe you and your sister can have play dates with him when you're all a bit bigger.

He chuckled. "Your mama blew me a kiss and that stuffy-looking department chair of hers winced. You'd think she spit on him or something."

Victor's grin faded. "The next day we were racing to the emergency room with preterm contractions. A shot of some horrible stuff that gave her the shakes helped get them under control, but then bed rest, which sounded fun until we realized... well, never mind about that, but suffice it to say it was good I started work at Thorndyke Associates a couple of weeks later. I bet your mama was bored out of her mind, but she never complained."

He glanced away from his intense scrutiny of his newborn son to take in the angelic face of the woman he loved. Again a smile creased his lips.

"Last night, after finally getting the go-ahead from the doctors, we went to see the fireworks. That was fun. And after... even more fun." His grin turned to a smirk. "Good thing, too, because she woke up an hour later having real contractions. By the time we called your grandma and made our way to the hospital, there wasn't much time left. It went that fast."

Victor swallowed hard at the intense memory. "Thank goodness for Mom—your grandma, that is— and her research on hypnobirthing and pressure points. I'm pretty sure her guided meditation and massage were all that got your mama through the rapid and painful hour between our arrival and… you, little man."

The baby blinked and opened his tiny mouth in a huge yawn, which promptly spurred Victor's own. "You're right. It was very tiring getting you born, and then, instead of being able to rest, we had to deliver your sister too. She's gonna be a sassy one, I bet. Barreled her way into the world with a shout! After that, your mama kind of… passed out. She wanted to feed you two right away, but she was too tired. So your grandma and I get to introduce ourselves to you two in the meanwhile."

Across the room, little Emily let out a noisy squawk to her grandmother, tattling on the delivery room nurses who'd had the effrontery to scrub her and put ointment in her eyes. She was most displeased by this impolite treatment and didn't hesitate to make her opinion known in a series of trembling howls. Oh, and she was also hungry and wanted her mother.

Roused by the baby's squeals, Caroline opened her eyes. She saw her husband sitting on the edge of the bed holding their son, his eyes shiny and full of love and wonder.

Turning toward the sound, she discovered her mother-in-law holding her daughter, tears rolling unchecked down her cheeks. "Sam?"

"Oh, you're awake, honey." The older woman wiped her eyes and stood. "I think your little girl needs you."

"Yes," Caroline more choked than said, tears clogging her throat.

Sam brought the baby to her.

Caroline struggled into a sitting position, wincing at the discomfort of her recent delivery, and placed a pillow on her lap. She lowered the front of her hospital gown and attempted to bring her daughter to her breast. It took a few tries, and Emily made it clear she did not appreciate the delay, but finally, she managed to position the little girl properly.

The baby quieted as she taught herself to eat.

"Oh, little teacher, look at you," Victor said, cradling their son against his chest and brushing a strand of short dark hair off Caroline's forehead with one hand. "You know, I dreamed about this day."

"You did?" Caroline tore her gaze away from the sight of her daughter—*finally a baby of my own*—to her husband.

"Yes," he admitted in a voice no steadier than her own, "you always were my dream come true."

Their eyes locked. A silent message of love beyond words passed between them. "And you were mine," she murmured into the silence. "Baby, let me see that little boy."

He scooted up close to her, showing her their son.

Caroline's breath caught at the sight of the tiny face. "Oh, Victor, he's precious. I love you. I love you all, so much!"

"I love you too, Caroline. *Te adoro, mi vida.*" He held up the baby so she could kiss him, and then he leaned in to receive his own kiss.

Our love already grows with every passing day, but today, it took a huge leap.

Hearts swelling, they kissed again. Victor helped Caroline position their son on her other breast so he could nurse too.

Joaquin took the fumbling stoically but once he was

in place, he released a pleased coo and settled in, quite happy to eat.

Caroline looked down at the children she had once feared she would never have. *It took so many years for me to find the love of my life, to get pregnant with his babies, but I no longer regret the delay.* Tears of joy spilled down her cheeks. *This beautiful moment was worth waiting for.*

AFTERWORD

Dear Readers,

Thank you for spending some time with Victor and Caroline. I hope you enjoyed this sweet, sexy romp. If you'd head over to my Amazon author page and leave me an honest review; complimentary or critical, long or short, even a couple of words, I'd really appreciate it.

I love to hear from my readers. Feel free to send me an email at

simonebeaudelaireauthor@hotmail.com.

Take care and keep reading romance!

Discover more books by Simone Beaudelaire at

https://www.nextchapter.pub/authors/simone-beaudelaire-romance-author.

Want to know when one of our books is free or discounted? Join the newsletter at http://eepurl.com/bqqB3H.

Love always,
Simone Beaudelaire

You could also like:
Baylee Breaking by Simone Beaudelaire

To read the first chapter for free, head to:
https://www.nextchapter.pub/books/baylee-breaking-contemporary-romance.

ABOUT THE AUTHOR

In the world of the written word, Simone Beaudelaire strives for technical excellence while advancing a worldview in which the sacred and the sensual blend into stories of people whose relationships are founded in faith but are no less passionate for it. Unapologetically explicit, yet undeniably classy, Beaudelaire's 20+ novels aim to make readers think, cry, pray... and get a little hot and bothered.

In real life, the author's alter-ego teaches composition at a community college in a small western Kansas town, where she lives with her four children, three cats, and husband—fellow author Edwin Stark.

As both romance writer and academic, Beaudelaire devotes herself to promoting the rhetorical value of the romance in hopes of overcoming the stigma associated with literature's biggest female-centered genre.

BOOKS BY SIMONE BEAUDELAIRE

When the Music Ends (The Hearts in Winter Chronicles Book 1)

When the Words are Spoken (The Hearts in Winter Chronicles Book 2)

Caroline's Choice (The Hearts in Winter Chronicles Book 3)

When the Heart Heals (The Hearts in Winter Chronicles Book 4)

The Naphil's Kiss

Blood Fever

Polar Heat

Xaman (with Edwin Stark)

Darkness Waits (with Edwin Stark)

Watching Over the Watcher

Baylee Breaking

Amor Maldito: Romantic Tragedies from Tejano Folklore

Keeping Katerina (The Victorians Book 1)

Devin's Dilemma (The Victorians Book 2)

Colin's Conundrum (The Victorians Book 3)

High Plains Holiday (Love on The High Plains Book 1)

High Plains Promise (Love on the High Plains Book 2)

High Plains Heartbreak (Love on the High Plains Book 3)

High Plains Passion (Love on the High Plains Book 4)

Devilfire (American Hauntings Book 1)

Saving Sam (The Wounded Warriors Book 1 with J.M. Northup)

Justifying Jack (The Wounded Warriors Book 2 with J.M. Northup)

Making Mike (The Wounded Warriors Book 3 with J.M

Northup)

Si tu m'Aimes (If you Love me)

Caroline's Choice
ISBN: 978-4-86745-680-4
Mass Market

Published by
Next Chapter
1-60-20 Minami-Otsuka
170-0005 Toshima-Ku, Tokyo
+818035793528

30th April 2021

CPSIA information can be obtained
at www.ICGtesting.com
Printed in the USA
LVHW040752170521
687631LV00012B/1057